MW01493500

Every time we help someone, it lessens the burden on Jesus.
Just like the man who helped Jesus carry the cross.

D Marie

Journey to the Noble Horse, is a wonderful middle-grade fiction based on biblical truths. This inspirational story takes place 400 years ago and drives home the character of God. Throughout the book the common thread of His character will allow you to reflect on your own journey as you grow your faith. As each character in this book walks their own journey through life's storms, forgiveness, and joy they learn how God is always the God of Hope. As a grandmother, I look forward to sharing this book with my 7 grandchildren.

Judi Bertels, CEO African Vision of Hope

As the father of three daughters, I am so thankful for the way D Marie creatively shares the heart of the Gospel through her storytelling. The truth that life isn't always easy, but there's always the hope of redemption. We have a saying at our church that when things look their worst, God is often up to His best. We see this over and over again throughout Scripture, and D Marie does a great job of sharing that truth in this work. And I know her words will greatly bless those who read them.

Andy Turner, Lead Minister, Leclaire Christian Church

Journey to the Noble Horse

Journey to the Noble Horse

D Marie

Illustrated by

Reverend Brian King

Copyright © 2020 by D Marie

All rights reserved. No part of this book may be used or reproduced by any means, graphic, electronic, or mechanical, including photocopying, recording, taping or by any information storage retrieval system without the written permission of the author except in the case of brief quotations embodied in critical articles and reviews.

Scripture taken from the King James Version of the Bible

This is the work of fiction. All of the characters, names, incidents, organizations, and dialogue in this novel are either the products of the author's imagination or are used fictitiously.

WWW.DMarieBooks.com

Certain stock imagery © Shutterstock
Certain stock imagery © Getty Images

ISBN: 978-1-7340520-3-9

Library of Congress Control Number: 2020912753

Printed in the United States of America

Dedication

Susan Marshall, first my sister,
forever my best friend
Our journey in life is filled with love

Special Acknowledgement

The Lord, my Banner, for the inspiration for this book

Contents

Introduction

Journey to the Noble Horse is part two in a trilogy that offers a Christian-based tale to model how faith and a personal relationship with the Lord can help overcome the trials of life. Prayers and Scriptures are woven into the story since such are fundamental in any relationship with God.

The story here begins where part one, Journey to the Glass Hill, ends. Ari was alone in his cooking room. Ari's wife, Johanna, (pronounced Yo-HAHN-nah) had died unexpectedly eighteen years before. Unable to cope with her death, he became bitter. His youngest son, Johann, (pronounced YO-hahn) looked too much like his mother, causing Ari pain and thus his desire to distance himself from this child. Magnus and Ivar (pronounced EE-var), Ari's favorite sons, became remorseful of their mistreatment of Johann after discovering and reading a hidden Bible. When they wanted to go to their brother and ask for forgiveness, Ari grew angry and told them not to come back home if they did.

Johann would now live in the palace, and Ari's oldest sons abandoned him. Despair overwhelmed Ari when he realized what had happened. Sitting down, he noticed a book, the Bible, on the table. Wondering if this was what had caused all the problems he faced now, he began to read.

The characters from part one join many more characters added to part two. Their lives are intertwined and have a profound influence on each other. The horse is symbolic of good. Even when it seems like we are alone when fighting oppression, the Lord is there in the midst of the battle.

Discussion starters for the chapters are located at the end of the book.

Enjoy the Journey,

D Marie

Chapter 1

Day of Trouble

A slight chill hung in the air, encouraging some of the leaves on the trees to surrender their green color. The setting sun painted the sky with shades of orange. Darkness spread into the house, and a lonely candle waited for a flame. Cold ashes lay in the fireplace while the empty kettle offered nothing to eat. The house was unoccupied except for Ari.

"What have I done?" he cried out. Pangs of agony tightened his chest. Tormenting thoughts invaded his mind. "Johanna, what have I done?"

Eighteen years had passed since the last time Ari had spoken her name aloud as she died in his arms. Losing his beloved wife had crushed his spirit. Now, he had lost the remaining part of his family.

Tilting his head upward, Ari squeezed his eyelids shut. Lines of pain filled his face. "Johanna, I have chased our sons away."

He buried his head in his arms atop the table. Lifting his head again, Ari cried out, "God forgive me! I have sinned against You, and I'm paying the price. I shouldn't have directed my anger toward You and shunned Johann when my Johanna died. Now, he's gone. I chased away Magnus and Ivar for wanting to seek forgiveness from Johann. Now, they're gone. All my sons are gone. I'm not worthy for You to listen to me, but I am sorry. Please forgive me."

Ari's attention drifted toward the opened book he had been reading—the same one that had so transformed Magnus' and

Ivar's hearts earlier that morning. He closed it. "God, Johanna always said, 'the Lord provides.' Please help me. Show me what You revealed to Magnus and Ivar. I want You. I want my sons back."

Resting the Bible on its spine, Ari slowly removed his hands. The worn pages parted and revealed the book of Psalms. "Lord, this is Your Book, Your Bible. Please show me the words You want me to learn." As Ari glanced at the page, his eyes focused on some of the words. They seemed larger and bolder than the other words:

> *Call upon Me in your day of trouble, and I will deliver you and you shall glorify Me.*

Ari lowered his head and pondered on those words. "Lord, this is my day of trouble, please deliver me."

The remaining light in the house faded away, the sun finally setting. His mind drifted to the previous night when his youngest son had climbed the glass hill for the third time. At daybreak, Johann had gone to the palace to return the three golden apples to the royal family, the reward for climbing the slippery slope. Now, Johann was betrothed to Princess Tea and would one day rule the kingdom of Christana.

The words Ari had told his oldest sons haunted him in the silence that permeated the house: "Don't come back if you seek forgiveness from Johann." Everyone had left him.

Pain tightened its grip around Ari's heart. Distress filled his mind. His eyes burned from the salty tears that would not cease to flow. Ari was reaping the consequences of his bitterness. He closed his eyes, laid his head on the Bible, and submitted himself to God. Soon, he drifted off to sleep.

While dreaming, he saw Johanna as she had been all those years ago. With a smile on her face, a song in her heart, and prayers on her lips, she played with her twin sons. Baby Johann lay in the cradle. Tired, Johanna sat down. She forced a smile for her sons. Exhausted by the playtime, she propped her head on her bent arm. Why was she so tired? Was the work too hard? Was there something wrong with her health? As Ari watched Johanna, he heard a knock on a door, but he remained quiet. The knock became more insistent. Again, he ignored the noise and quietly watched Johanna. This time, the knock became a pounding noise, and Ari woke up.

"Ari!" the voice behind the door yelled, "Are you there?"

Ari raised his head off the table and shook it to clear the dream away. "Johanna?"

"Lars," the voice replied.

"Lars?" Ari softly repeated. Finally, his mind cleared enough to realize that the minister was knocking on the door.

"Ari?" the voice asked. "Are you all right?"

"Yes, please, come on in."

Lars opened the door and found a groggy looking man sitting at his table. Occasional strands of gray hid in his brown, curly hair. Two or more days of stubble protruded on his normally clean-shaven face. One side of his face bore a redden area. Perhaps from his head laying on the table all night. "I'm here, Lord; guide me through this," Lars quietly prayed. With a hearty smile and comforting voice, Lars began the conversation, "Good morning, Ari! How are you today?" Not giving Ari a chance to reply, Lars continued, "I woke up very early this morning and fixed too much food. I thought I'd share it with someone. Do you like porridge?"

"Yes," Ari mumbled—the extent of his current conversational skills. He blinked his eyes as he focused on the opened doorway and noticed the darkness outside being consumed by the rising sun.

"Good!" replied Lars. He reached into his basket, lifted up two bowls of porridge, and placed them on the table. Glancing around the cooking room, the silver-haired man laid his crossed arms on his rotund midsection. His eyes sparkled as he walked to the hearth and retrieved two spoons. Taking a deep breath, he sat down across from Ari. "Let's ask for the Lord's blessing for our meal." Ari stared blankly while the minister continued, "Lord, we come before You with humble hearts and ask You to bless this food. We lift up Your name and praise You. We ask for Your guidance in our lives. In Your name, we pray. Amen."

"Amen," Ari added. "Lars...uh, *Reverend* Lars," he corrected himself, "I have sinned, and I'm so sorry. I asked God to forgive me, but I don't know what to do to make amends."

"You already have, Ari. When you repented, asking God for forgiveness, the Lord forgave you immediately."

"But what about the people I've hurt?" Ari's eyes drifted down toward the table.

"Ari, when someone offends you and say they're sorry, would you forgive them?"

"It depends if they really meant it. Actions speak louder than words. I guess the level of the forgiveness depends on the level of how much the person is truly sorry and wants to correct the situation." Lifting his head, Ari continued, "But, that attitude can lead to holding a grudge. I have lived with bitterness too long. I don't want to carry it in my soul any longer. I want to forgive regardless if the person is sincere or not. Most importantly, I want to be forgiven. If I can't do it by myself, then I'll ask God for strength."

"Perfect answer!" Lars said with a hearty smile. "When you see your sons, follow your own advice. Trust God, and trust your sons."

Lars sympathetically watched as Ari closed his eyes and took a deep breath. "Ari, I have good news! I saw Magnus and Ivar yesterday. They want to become ministers of the Lord. They met with Johann. Your sons are reunited. All is well. Johann wants his brothers to perform his wedding ceremony when they finish their training. Johann has offered Magnus and Ivar the minister's position and has given them Elina's cottage."

Pondering on Lars' words, the broken man remained silent.

Ari's sorrowful face gnawed at Lars' heart and he placed his wrinkled hand on Ari's weathered hand. "Ari, your sons are returning, and they'll live here, once again, by you. And Ari, I'm here for you. Come and see me anytime you want."

"Thank you, Reverend," Ari replied, "you have helped me already. I'll return your dishes."

"Anytime, Ari. My door is always open. I must leave now. I have some people waiting for me."

Lars walked outside closing the door as he left. Placing his hand on the doorpost, he prayed. "Lord, let Your will be done." His horse neighed loudly and nodded as if he agreed.

Ari stood up and paced the floor. He stopped, looked toward the ceiling and cried out to the Lord, "Jesus, take me just as I am, a sinner. Forgive me and heal my heart. If I have never asked You before, I am asking now. Come into my life."

He closed his eyes and focused on those words. As he meditated, he thought he heard a loud thud. Looking around, he saw nothing unusual, but he felt different. A binding chain had just been loosened from his head and dropped to the ground. He opened the front door to see if the noise came from that direction. Lars was long gone. While he stood by the door, he envisioned the chain being dragged through the doorway and taken outside. Quickly, he closed the door.

A lightness flowed into Ari. A peace that he had never experienced before. He felt so much better that he simply had to tell Lars immediately. Going to his room, Ari changed clothes and cleaned himself up. Looking in the mirror, he saw the lines of agony being replaced by the glow of joy. A smile resided on his face. The pressure in his brain disappeared. Ari felt freed from the bitterness he had been carrying for eighteen years. He stopped for a moment. "How do I tell Lars about what just happened?" His eyes narrowed in on the bowls of porridge sitting on the table. "I'll tell him when I return his bowls. Lars said his door was always open."

While pouring the porridge into one of his own bowls, Ari noticed something wedged between the last pages of the Bible.

He pulled out a cloth with a cross on it. Clutching it with his hands, he raised his arms. "Lord, this will be my banner. I'll take it with me everywhere I go."

Ari quickly wrapped Lars' bowls in a different cloth, tied the ends together, and headed for the barn. His feet barely touched the ground.

The horse nodded and whinnied when Ari gently rubbed his neck as if the large animal sensed a change in his master's touch. He patiently waited while Ari prepared him for riding.

Sitting tall in the saddle with bowls in hand, Ari took a deep breath and rode down the lane. Approaching the square, he noticed other horses in front of the church. *What's going on?* he wondered. "It's Sunday, the Lord's day. Lars had to get back for the church service."

Ari secured his horse's reins to the rail. Taking a deep breath, he eyed the church door, contemplating his next move. "Lars said his door was always open." Scrunching his eyebrows together, he walked into the church carrying the bowls still wrapped in the cloth. Ari looked straight ahead and recognized the man standing by the baptismal font.

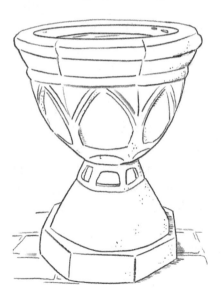

The man had been the male witness to his twin sons' baptism. Oscar's brown hair had streaks of gray, but he still looked the same. Lars was almost finished baptizing Oscar's grandson when he saw Ari entering the church.

The minister poured water on the child as he said the words, "In the name of the Father, the Son, and the Holy Spirit." Lars focused on Ari and continued to pour water on the baby. Oscar pulled his grandson away from the baptismal font for the child was getting drenched.

Ari's heart pounded in his chest. "Johann's here. I can feel it," he murmured as he scanned the crowd until he found his son. Breathing deeply, he summoned the courage to announce his presence, "Reverend, I'm here to return your dishes." At this declaration, everyone in the church turned around to look at him. "You said your door is always open." Ari walked down the aisle with the banner in one hand and the cloth covered bowls in the other. He gave the bowls to the first person he passed.

The royal family had also turned around to see who had entered the church. Johann sat at the end next to Princess Tea. He raised his eyebrows as he saw the man at the back of the church. Tea noticed and gently squeezed his hand.

Johann's blue eyes followed his father as he walked down the aisle clutching the banner in his hand. "Father found the Bible," he whispered.

"Reverend, I want to see my son."

Johann's mouth dropped open. Tea squeezed his hand even harder. By this time, Ari had walked to the front of the church. King Albert and Queen Maria intently watched Ari. Did they need to protect Johann, their daughter's betrothed?

Johann's heart raced as he stared at his father. His dry throat caused him to gulp.

Ari walked closer to Johann studying his son's face no longer seeing his deceased wife, just his fair-haired son. Johann's wavy hair laid in layers. His soft blue eyes spoke of no ill will. In the matter of days, his son had transformed from a child to a young man.

Ari's voice cracked as he spoke, "Johann, my son, I've been so wrong. I'll spend the rest of my life giving you the love a father has for his son. Please forgive me."

Johann's heart kept pounding in his chest. "I forgive you, Papa," he replied and extended his hand. Ari grabbed it, pulled his son up into his arms, and hugged his neck. Johann surrendered to the embrace and laid his head on his father's broad shoulders as they both wept. King Albert's hands trembled as he raised his hands up high and thanked the Lord. He had never given up seeking God's help for this family. Although it took many years, his prayer had been answered.

The congregation watched in awe. There wasn't a dry eye in the whole church. Oscar guided his family back to their pew while Lars remained by the baptismal font. At least he had finally stopped pouring water.

Ari turned his attention to Lars. "Reverend, I don't know if I have ever been baptized. I want to be certain, and I want to be baptized today, now."

Tea stood up. "I'll be your witness."

Ari looked at her with amazement. Tea's curly golden tresses extended past her shoulders and framed the graceful features of her face. Her grayish-blue eyes reflected a joyful spirit. Although Ari stood a head taller than Tea, the small framed, young woman displayed an air of confidence coupled with charm. *This young woman, who is the love of Johann's life, wants to do this for me?* he thought. "Thank you, Princess Tea," Ari replied bowing his head. He pronounced her name as TAY-uh. "You are beautiful and kind."

"It is my honor to be your witness, Papa," Johann said, keeping his eyes on his father. His prayer had been answered today, and he softly said, "The Lord provides."

Ari heard him and responded, "Yes, Son, He does provide. I'm beginning to understand those words."

Reverend Lars called for the three to come forward. There was no doubt in Ari's mind now. He was baptized into the promises of God. He raised his arms in the air and proclaimed, "Thank You, Lord."

This would be a Sunday no one would forget. As time went by, the sermon might not be remembered, but this family reunion and baptism would never be forgotten.

Chapter 2

The Invitation

Lars concluded the Sunday service. A hush spread through the crowd of parishioners. They watched every move King Albert made before they approached Ari to congratulate him.

The king, who stood head-to-head with Ari, projected a demeanor that was regal but approachable. His square jawline conveyed a persona of dignity and strength that was complimented by his graying blond hair. He privately said a few words to his wife who smiled and nodded. Ari wiped his clammy hands on his pants. His eyes followed Maria as she took Tea's hand and guided her to the narthex where they stopped.

Ari's stomach churned. *What's the king going to do to me?* he pondered. *I haven't treated Johann kindly. Will King Albert make me pay for my actions?*

Johann escorted his father to where the king stood. Ari bowed. When he straightened, King Albert smiled and extended both arms to him. "Ari, welcome to the family."

Ari's knees nearly buckled, and he gulped in disbelief. His dry mouth did manage to utter, "Thank you, Your Highness."

"Ari, you and Johann will want some time together," Albert continued. "Please join us for our midday meal."

"Thank you, King Albert." Ari slowly rubbed his clammy hands on his pants again. "You are very kind."

Albert smiled and nodded. Out of the corner of his eye, he caught sight of a somewhat familiar face. The man glared and quickly exited the church. By the time Albert reached the door, the man was gone.

Maria walked to his side. "Something wrong?"

"I thought I saw someone I knew from a long time ago," Albert replied guardedly.

"From Christana?" Maria asked.

"No, from Herrgott. He's gone. Let's get Tea and go home."

While Albert was leaving, extended hands of the remaining congregants came from all directions to greet Ari and give their best wishes. His worst fear disintegrated. *I'm not being rejected. They're not holding my past behavior against me. I'm forgiven.*

Oscar waited outside with his sons to speak with Ari about a business proposition. Benjamin and Klaus both agreed with what their father intended to do. Seeing Ari exiting the church, Oscar greeted him, "Ari, congratulations! Remember when I was the witness for Magnus' and Ivar's baptism? I mentioned then that I hoped they would help me with my horses someday, but since they have chosen a different calling, I've got a different proposition. Would you be interested in having my two sons work for you? They have some knowledge of horses, and perhaps they could help you at your farm."

Ari's eyes widened. His heart raced. "Yes, that would be wonderful. I want to go see my other sons as soon as possible. After I train your sons, they could take care of my farm while I'm gone. When I return, I'll teach them all the skills I know and share the profits with them."

"Wonderful!" Oscar exclaimed. "As you saw today, my eldest son, Benjamin, has a new member in his family to provide for. My youngest son, Klaus, isn't married. Both want to learn the horse trade. When do you want them to start?"

"Is tomorrow too soon?"

"Benjamin told me that he could be released from his current position right away. Both will be there at first light."

"Thank you. I'll be waiting in the morning." Ari grabbed Oscar's hand and shook it vigorously. Looking over at Johann,

Ari's face fell. He recalled his treatment of his youngest. *This is the boy I made do the work with no encouragement or pay.*

Johann reached for his father's hand and squeezed it. "Papa, I want you to know, before we go into the palace, that I love you. I always have, and I always will."

Tears welled in Ari's eyes and then ran down his cheeks when he closed them. With a deep sigh he said, "Lord, I thank You for my son." He opened his eyes and wiped his face. "When you were born, I asked your mother if we could name you Johann. Johanna said you would be her gift to me—and you are."

Johann wept. Their tears produced a medicinal effect and washed away the repressed emotions and allowed the Lord to fill them with His grace.

With horse in tow, Ari walked with Johann to the palace. Ari watched the guards bow to his son. Entering the doors, he suddenly recalled that Johann had lived there as a child.

Ari surveyed the surroundings of the inner courtyard while Johann asked a stableman to take charge of his father's horse. The man nodded to Johann but squinted his dark brown eyes at Ari. As he walked closer to retrieve the horse's reins, Ari noticed a scar on the side of the caretaker's face, a rather long scar that ran along the edge of his beard. Gunther's shoulder length hair partially hid the scar when he lowered his head. Although he lacked the same height as Ari, his frame was every bit as muscular.

"Thank you, sir," Ari told the caretaker. The man remained silent and bowed his head. An odd feeling drifted by Ari. He dismissed the thought and turned to the courtyard. Flower gardens and fountains graced the open space. Symmetrically designed paths guided the observer to all the areas. Numerous trees offered shade and rest. Strategically placed statues enhanced the visual interest. Fishponds provided tranquility.

Ari remembered the chicken manure the palace wanted for a garden and chuckled. "Where was the…" he started to say.

Perceiving his question, Johann pointed to a nearby garden

where beautiful flowers grew. "Over there, Papa."

Entering the palace, Ari's eyes roamed the hallways absorbing the amazing sights. Suspended chandeliers held lit candles. Colorful woven tapestries, hanging on the walls, displayed scenes from the king's family life. Several chairs surrounded the dining table. He smelled tantalizing aromas floating through the air. Impeccably dressed servants stood in a row near the table and waited for their cue to serve.

King Albert took his place at the end of the table with Queen Maria sitting to his right. Princess Tea sat next to her mother. Albert motioned for Ari to sit in the seat of honor next to him, and Johann sat next to his father. Memories of Johann serving food began to flood Ari's mind.

With a sorrowful look on his face, Ari turned to his son. "Johann, I'm so sorry for—"

Johann immediately interrupted. He looked at his father, shook his head, and replied, "Papa, I forgave you. I forgave you for everything. Let us learn from our past, but let's not allow the past to interfere with our future."

Maria looked at Albert and quietly squeezed his hand. Johann had tempered love with wisdom, traits of a good future king.

Albert clapped his hands, and the servants came forward with the food. Looking at the full plate, Albert folded his hands.

"Let's all bow our heads and give thanks to the Lord. Father, we ask for Your blessing on this food, and we give You thanks. We thank You for the gift of Ari. He's Your son whom You love so much that You gave Your only Son, Jesus, to die for us so we may have eternal life with You. In Your name, we pray. Amen."

Ari's mouth gaped open. His brain spun as he took in the reality of the situation. Not only did God forgive him, but his son and his king did, too.

"Ari," King Albert began with a knowing smile, "you're what sometimes is referred to as a baby Christian. Just take small steps and observe what people do. If they are Christian, you will feel it in your soul. It's a positive feeling. If they are not, the Lord sends you subtle, uncomfortable feelings. Trust God."

"King Albert," Ari started, but Albert raised his hand and stopped him.

"Ari, you're family. You may address us by our first names when we're together. When we're not together and you are referring about us to others, it's different. In respect to the position of the crown, proper referral is to use the term, the king, or the full title, King Albert. The same reference is for Maria and Tea."

Tiny smile lines appeared at the corners of Maria's soft gray eyes as she looked at Ari. Her face glowed with charm reflecting similar features that she shared with her daughter. Tightly curled brown hair, partially secured behind her head, hung in ringlets barely touching her shoulders.

"Ari, we have only met one time, the day Albert and I were married. I had many opportunities to be with Elina, your mother-by-marriage, during the time she and Johann stayed here at the palace. She always talked fondly of you. You were the closest person she ever had to a son. I know what she felt. Albert and I only have one child, Tea, so Johann is like a son to us. We're blessed to have him as Tea's betrothed. Albert never had a brother as he's an only child. We welcome you and want you to become part of our family."

This time Albert squeezed her hand. "Well said, my love. Now, let's eat or the food will be cold."

Ari turned toward Johann. Scrunching his eyebrows together he scrutinized the empty plates laid out in front of the unoccupied chairs. Albert noticed. "Uh, Ari, the members of the court will be arriving later to meet Johann. Our time right now is just for family."

Ari breathed a sigh of relief and nodded hoping he hadn't intruded.

After the meal, everyone stood up. Tea walked over and stood by Johann's side. She looked at Ari and shared, "I'm so happy to be with you. Johann has many fond memories that he has shared with me about his adventures on the farm. I would love to come and see it. I especially would like to see the horses."

"Tea," Ari responded, "I look forward to showing you my farm and to preparing a meal for you. I must confess, I'm not a very good cook."

At this point, Albert walked up to Ari and said, "Ari, have you ever wondered how those horses Johann rode were able to climb the glass hill when the other horses couldn't even get their hoofs to stay on the glass?"

Ari's eyes grew large. "Yes, Magnus, Ivar, and I all wondered. We have never seen this breed before."

"Johann, let me walk with your father for a while. I have something to show him," Albert requested.

"Certainly, Albert," replied Johann. "Tea and I will be in the library."

"See you later, Son," Ari said. Then, he faced the queen. "Maria, thank you for all your kind words."

Maria nodded. "You're welcome."

Chapter 3

Secret Revealed

Tall trees blocked their view of the shared wall separating the palace grounds and the horses. Albert guided Ari to the path that led to the pasture and stable. Passing the trees, Ari stared at the top of the glass hill. His eyes followed the plain, wooden steps descending to the bottom of the wall to the inside of the courtyard.

A guard opened the large wooden door that revealed what was left of the glass hill. Workers busied themselves with the dismantling of the thick glass covering the artificial hill under the direction of the glass artisan. His stern face stayed focused on each action as they carried the large blocks of glass, wrapped in leather, and loaded them in the wagon. The glass would be melted again to make windowpanes.

Albert paused for a few moments to allow Ari to take in the enormity of the project. "Ready to see the horses?"

"I'm ready," Ari replied.

Ari marveled at the royal stable. Smooth stones paved the floors. Each horse had an immaculate stall to accommodate their needs. They had plenty of room to walk, eat, and lay down. Clean straw covered the stall floors. Ari mentally compared the royal stalls to his. *I better get them cleaned up before Tea comes for a visit.*

Some of the horses seemed content despite their long stay in the stable. Several horses pawed at the ground eager to run in the pasture again. Once the glass was completely removed, they would be free to roam the grassy field.

At the end of the stable, Albert slowed down and stopped

walking. Ari peered into the stall and saw the brown horse that Johann had ridden in his first attempt to scale the glass hill. Walking a little more, he saw the black horse. Finally, the last stall contained the white horse. Being in the presence of these prized horses rendered Ari speechless. He visualized each one of them climbing the hill of glass.

"Ari," Albert began, "they're all the same breed, called Edelross. They change colors as they get older. It takes a special breed and training to get them to jump the way they did as they approached the hill. That jump gave them the advantage to get past the slippery glass at the base of the glass hill. Would you like to ride one?"

"Yes!"

Albert nodded to the nearby caretaker who kept his face turned away from Ari. Ari frowned. The king said, "Ari, this is Gunther. He will help us."

Gunther bowed to the king, revealing the scar Ari had noted from before, and proceeded to prepare the white horse. After the Edelross was tacked and ready, Gunther led the horse out of the stables behind the king and Ari.

"You won't be able to leave the enclosed pasture," Albert said, "but you'll be able to tell a difference immediately with this breed."

Even with all his years with horses, Ari was a little intimidated by this one. *Johann could do this with no experience of riding. This should be easy,* he told himself. Still, there was something special about the horse. He placed his foot in the stirrup and mounted the magnificent steed. Ari felt the might of the horse's muscular body, a strong but controlled strength.

Talking to the steed in his normal voice, the horse turned his head and looked Ari in the eye. "I think he's planning something."

"Hold on tight!" warned Albert.

Suddenly, the horse bolted for the glass hill. The workers saw the horse and rider approaching and scrambled out of the way. The horse stopped, reared up on his hind legs, and started to jump on the hill. Ari gasped, his eyes widening. It took all his strength to stay in the saddle and steer the horse away from the dangerous surface. Using every skill he possessed to calm the horse, Ari redirected the stallion back to the stable.

"I think you two had enough exercise for one day," Albert said with a slight smile.

Gunther waited until Ari dismounted before coming forward to retrieve the horse. Quietly, the stable hand guided the horse back to his stall to curry and feed him some extra grain.

"Amazing," Ari managed to say. "I have never seen a horse react like that before. Thank you for letting me ride him."

"You're welcome, Ari. The horses' abilities allowed them to jump past the slippery base of the hill," Albert shared. "The next level of glass is very thick. It is scored and has wood embedded in it for secure footing. This allowed the horses to climb the hill. Only the white one could reach the top due to his strength and endurance." The king paused, his eyes twinkling mischievously. "Would you like to know how we delivered the horses to your farm without being detected?" Albert asked.

"Yes." Ari quickly replied.

"Gunther rode each horse to Elina's cottage and secured it in the back. The clothes were already in the cottage. When the time was right, he switched the ordinary saddle and reins to the adorned saddle and reins. Then, he brought the horse and clothes over after you left the farm. When Johann returned, Gunther retrieved the horse and clothes, changed the saddle and reins, and rode the stallion back to the palace. He did this all three nights."

"A well thought out plan."

"Eligible suitors in Christana were given an opportunity to be awarded the horse. But sadly, Johann was the only one who demonstrated the character of a good king when I went around the town in my beggar-man disguise. Gunther and two more of my guards wore the disguises, too. Their results were the same as mine."

Ari lowered his head, ashamed of his twin son's treatment of Albert when he had come disguised as a beggar-man to the farm. Albert sensed it.

"Ari," Albert said reassuringly, "take heart. The Lord had a plan for all of your sons. Their behavior was used, and they are now working for His good."

"Thank you, Albert," Ari said with woeful eyes. "How can I ever repay you?"

"We're family. There will be family matters that we can both help each other with." Ari smiled at this good assurance.

"Come. Johann will want to spend more time with you before the sun sets."

Questions about the horses rumbled in Ari's mind, but he refrained from asking the king. It would have to wait until another time. *Hopefully, I'll be able to learn the skills used to train these horses. I wonder who did the training. Was it Gunther?*

Johann and Ari spent the remainder of the afternoon with each other. The time passed too quickly, and Ari needed to return home.

"Papa, if you need help with the farm, I'll be there."

"Son, I truly appreciate your wanting to help, but your place is here. Albert will have many things for you to learn. You have an important destiny—a destiny that only a king can prepare you for. The kingdom of Christana and its people need you to learn those lessons well. You have a good heart, Johann. You'll be a great sovereign."

"Thank you, Papa." I have a gift for you." Johann removed the necklace and locket from his neck and gave it to his father. "Grandma gave this to me. She told me to place it over my heart. I could feel the warmth of her love and the Lord's love every time I laid my hand on top of my heart."

Ari stared at Johann. He held out his hand to receive the locket. The locket looked like the one Johanna had given the king and queen on their wedding day. *Elina had one, too,* he thought.

"Thank you, Son," Ari replied admiring the locket. "I'll wear it always. It will remind me of your love and the Lord's love."

With a cold glare watching the two, Gunther approached with Ari's horse. Ari bowed his head. "Thank you, sir, for taking care of my horse. You are most kind."

For the first time, Gunther offered a slight smile. He nodded toward Ari and returned to the stable. The uneasy feeling about this man faded a little. Ari mounted his horse and waved farewell to his son. During the ride home, Ari reminisced about the day's events from the moment Lars knocked on his door until leaving the palace. "I was forgiven, baptized, and surrounded with love today. Thank you, Jesus. You never gave up on me." He hummed a cheerful tune on his ride home. Closer to home, he focused his thoughts on his farm. "No fire in the fireplace, the animals have not been fed, and I have Oscar's sons coming at first light. I better get busy."

Chapter 4

Horse Training

The sun dipped below the horizon. When the moon finally appeared, it barely illuminated the sky. Ari shivered in the cool night air. He rubbed his aching arm after he had made several trips carrying a lantern in one hand and feed buckets in his other hand. Wiping the sweat off his forehead, he headed for the well to draw another bucket of water for his horses and chickens.

After tending his livestock, Ari's mind turned to the next necessary chore, and he proceeded to the woodpile. He thought of the cold hearth, unused these last two days. He'd need something to get a fire started. "Need kindling," he muttered, scraping together some of the twigs and shavings to take inside.

Upon entering the cooking room, Ari noticed the Bible on the table. "The banner!" he exclaimed. "Where did I put it?" He mentally retraced his steps. His last recollection of it was in the church. "It must be there. I'll go at first light. No, Oscar's sons are arriving then." Frustrated and exhausted, Ari turned his back and went to bed.

The knocking at the door vibrated in his ears. The morning's first light streamed through the window. Ari opened his eyes. He'd overslept. "Not again," he whispered. He quickly stood and readied himself. "Come in," he shouted.

The young men did not comment on his late rising. They looked around and went to work. Benjamin pushed back his walnut colored hair while narrowing his matching brown eyes as he looked for a fire starter. Finding the iron bar and flint, he struck enough sparks to light the kindling. Although the brothers were similar in height, Benjamin had a more mature muscular frame.

The younger brother, Klaus, had a ruddy complexion that glowed from his work outdoors tending the farmers' fields and animals. His brown eyes sparkled when he smiled which garnered some occasional teasing. Klaus wore his hair longer than his brother perhaps hoping his brown locks would conceal his boyish looks.

After Klaus gathered up the dirty dishes, he poured water and oat grain into the kettle. Benjamin removed a folded cloth from his pocket and laid it on the clean table while Klaus stirred the porridge.

When Ari came into the cooking room, he stopped in amazement. The brothers worked efficiently without any direction. Then, he looked at the table, and his eyes lit up. "You found my banner!"

"I found it in the church," Benjamin replied. "When I went back to get my son's blanket, I saw your banner on a pew."

Peace flowed into Ari. *Thank you, Lord, for providing the*

right young men to help me, he thought. "Thank you," he said aloud to the brothers.

They both smiled and nodded. As they sat at the table, Ari went over the general procedures of the farm with them. The two brothers listened intently. They inhaled the food, anxious to begin their new occupation.

A gust of chilly air greeted the three on their way to the barn. Once inside, the men mucked the stalls and replenished them with clean straw. Ari straightened his back and wiped the sweat from his forehead. He handed a bucket to each brother and pointed to the troughs.

Ari noticed his new helpers' wistful looks as they gazed outside at the horses, but he led Benjamin and Klaus to the coop to feed the chickens instead. Next, the garden needed tending. Only a few vegetables still hung on the vines or remained in the ground. After placing the vegetables in the lauder, Ari asked, "Do you want to rest first or work with the horses?"

Benjamin turned and grinned at Klaus. The brothers raced each other to the corral.

Ari led three horses into the enclosure. "Be careful of the black stallion. I suspect he allowed Johann to ride him, but he does not want anyone to bother him. He stays on the farm. Now, let's start at the beginning."

Ari hooked up a lead rope to a horse's halter and led him to the training arena. After finishing the rigorous course, Ari paused being out of breath. He glanced at the brothers while they watched him gasping for air.

The horse had to maneuver over several obstacles. Some obstacles required jumping over a hedge of bushes, a fence, or a ditch. Other obstacles required careful walking on uneven surfaces, like down a ledge of dirt or paved stones butted together, and maneuvering between three logs laying on the ground.

After watching Ari take the horse through the course once, Benjamin asked, "May I have a try?"

"Yes," Ari replied still panting for air.

Benjamin went to the corral and chose one of the two remaining horses. Determined to succeed, he approached the training course with a clenched jaw. He could run fast and keep pace with the horse, but he became winded when he finished the first lap. Next, it was Klaus' turn. After the last hurdle, Klaus looked at his teacher. Ari nodded his approval.

"Benjamin, Klaus, good work. Let's call in the other ones."

Klaus poured grain into the trough while Ari walked toward the gate. The horses' ears perked up at the sound of Ari's piercing whistle, and they headed for the corral.

The sun hovered over their heads. Ari was so involved with the camaraderie of his help that he didn't notice it was time for the midday meal.

Benjamin looked up and saw his father riding down the lane. "Papa," he called out, "we're over here."

Oscar got off his horse and stood by Ari. His chest puffed out watching his sons training the horses. "Well done!" he exclaimed.

"Papa," Klaus asked, "is that Mama's cooking I smell?"

"There's nothing wrong with your nose, Son," Oscar replied. "Mama, sent all of you something to eat."

"Ari," Klaus added, "you're in for a treat. Mama's a good cook."

"Splendid! Let's wash up and eat," Ari said.

Oscar and Ari took a short walk around the farm while the young men took the food inside. "Ari," Oscar began, "you want to go see Magnus and Ivar. It's a long journey to get there. If I may suggest, do not travel alone. Even Jesus sent His disciples out by twos. There's safety in numbers. Take Benjamin with you. Klaus can take care of the farm while you are gone. If you like, he can stay here at night to give your animals extra safekeeping."

"Oscar, you're very kind," Ari replied. "Let's ask if they want to do this."

Benjamin beamed with delight. "I would love to see the

kingdom with the University. I have never traveled far from Christana, and this would be an exciting adventure."

Klaus had never been away from his parent's home before. His eyes widened as he thought about this new opportunity of personally overseeing the farm, and he tried to suppress his boyish grin. "I do have one request," he said. "Someday, I would like to go to Herrgott."

"I will take you," promised Ari.

"Good," said Oscar. "Ari, when you are ready, I'll have my wife prepare food for the two of you to take on your journey. Right now, I have to get back to my new job with the carpenter. We have a large order of window frames for the glassmaker."

Johann rode up in front of the barn passing Oscar in the lane. "Papa," he yelled.

Ari smiled. "My day keeps getting better."

After listening to his father's plans, Johann commented, "Be careful on this journey. Albert has talked about this territory. Some parts have no protection. I'm relieved you're not traveling alone. Now, let's see how the horses are doing. Working with them was the highlight of my day." Johann had more to share but wanted to wait until it was time for his father to leave.

The horse whinnied and nodded when Johann picked up a lead rope and hooked it to the halter. Johann affectionately rubbed the animal's neck on the way to the training course. Not watching his step, his foot slipped on a patch of grass and he fell. His faced warmed up while he looked around to see who may have seen him fall.

At sunset, Johann, Benjamin, and Klaus returned to their homes. Ari organized the cooking room for the following day. Thoughts of quickly training Klaus rumbled through his mind. Visions of Magnus and Ivar warmed his heart.

"Tonight, I'm going to bed early. Two days in a row I have been oversleeping. Tomorrow, I will be ready."

Chapter 5

Preparations

Darkness still coated the sky when Ari woke up. He trudged to the hearth. Muffling a yawn, he gathered the embers together and added more firewood. Looking out the cooking room window, he saw two horses tethered to the rail in front of the barn. Benjamin and Klaus had arrived before first light. Ari walked across the yard to the barn. He kept out of view, but he could hear the two young men talking affectionately to the horses as they prepared them for the exercise course.

Klaus already had a lead rope on a horse and was rubbing the horse's neck on both sides. The rising sun offered more illumination, and Ari watched while the young man guided the mare through the course of obstacles. Ari admired Klaus' attention to detail. Benjamin patiently waited with the next horse.

Ari stepped out from behind a tree and approached the arena. "Great handling skills. You two are naturals. Today, I want you to reverse the direction on the course. This is one of my trade secrets. Please keep it that way. You must train both sides of the horse's brain. That's why it's important for the horse to accept your touch on both sides of their body."

Benjamin and Klaus locked eyes, silently acknowledging their inclusion into Ari's private information.

"There are three more unhaltered horses that need to be added to this group when I get back. Then, I'll teach you how to gently saddle break the haltered horses," Ari added.

Both of the brothers' hearts raced while unconsciously

wetting their lips. Ari had a special technique for this procedure. His best trade secret would become theirs, too.

"Ari, the barn was too dark when we arrived. We'll get busy on it now," Benjamin said.

Ari gave them a knowing smile. "You like horses as much as I do. Let's go inside."

Oscar returned at midday with more prepared food. "You're spoiling me, Oscar," Ari said inhaling the pleasant aroma.

"You've blessed my family. This is the least I can do to show my gratitude."

"Oscar, I have watched Klaus. He seems capable of handling the needs of the animals," Ari said. He then paused to take a deep breath. "When would you feel comfortable leaving Klaus by himself to take care of the farm?"

"I listened to him last night. He feels ready," Oscar replied. "Let's do this. Tomorrow, come to town and replenish your supplies. Benjamin will stay with me. Klaus can work your farm by himself. At the end of the day, you can judge if he can handle the work."

"Splendid idea."

For the rest of the day, Ari and Benjamin hauled water, chopped wood, and did any necessary maintenance work. Klaus worked only with the animals. After the brothers left, Ari opened his Bible and read the Gospel of Luke. Closing his eyes, he created a visual image of Jesus standing with His arms opened wide. The vision produced a comforting peace flowing inside of him. Ari relaxed so much that he nodded off. Startled, he woke up, closed the Book, and retired for the night.

The following morning, Ari noticed only one horse tethered to the barn rail. A large bundle rested on the horse's saddle. He found Klaus already tending the chores. Klaus glanced at Ari. "Enjoy your day in Christana, and I'll enjoy my day here."

"Thank you," Ari replied.

Ari proceeded to get the wagon ready, but the horses were already hitched up and waiting for him. Klaus smiled and waved good-bye.

On his ride to the town, Ari took mental notes on how much food, clothing, and bedding he needed for travel. His mind search for possible ways to take his Bible. "Too big to pack. I'll copy a few verses and take them with me."

Maneuvering through the town square, Ari absently noticed the sentries standing in front of the palace. One of them disappeared into the palace after spotting Ari, so he was unsurprised when Johann came running to meet him a few minutes later.

Johann accompanied his father making his rounds in the shops. The aroma of something appetizing caught their attention and drew them into the inn where they talked for hours. Neither one of them noticed the innkeeper strumming his fingers on his service table and yawning at the same time.

Ari looked up and noticed that the other patrons had left. "I may be leaving tomorrow, Son. I'll come and see you as soon as I return. I love you, Johann."

Johann reached into his pocket and gave his father two letters. Ari grinned at the sight of Magnus' and Ivar's names. The second one looked different. It was secured with the official wax seal of King Albert. He flipped it over and read the recipient's name.

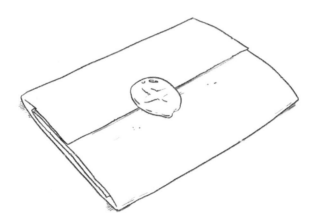

"Please deliver these for me."

"I will." Ari tucked the letters inside his shirt.

"Albert says the path crosses over to the east side of the Herrgott River when you enter the other country. There's a ferry that can help you cross the river about three days journey from here. Then, it's three more days to Herrgott where Magnus and Ivar are staying. Once you get to Herrgott, you'll have to cross the river again."

"Why do you cross the river twice?" Ari asked frowning.

"The undefined trail past the ferry on the east side can be perilous where two rivers converge. The west side is better. I'll pray for your safe journey and your speedy return, Papa."

"Not to worry, Son. I'll be home soon."

Ari mounted the wagon and guided his team of horses home. When he returned, Klaus' horse was gone.

"He went home," Ari muttered. He turned around and noticed wisps of smoke rising from the chimney and smiled. After hitching the team to the rail, Ari walked through the barn, noting its condition. He continued his inspection outside. "Hmm," he muttered. Retrieving the supplies, he approached his house inhaling something wonderful.

"Hello," greeted Klaus. "The food will be ready in a few minutes. Did you get everything you needed?"

"Yes," Ari replied. He noticed that the bundle that had been on Klaus' horse was now resting near the hearth.

"If it's all right with you, I put my belongings in your house. If you are comfortable with me staying here, you can start your journey tomorrow. With the daylight getting shorter, you may want to leave at first light when Benjamin gets here.

"The farm looks good, but are you sure about this, Klaus? You'll be here by yourself."

"I talked with Papa earlier, and I told him I'm ready." Klaus paused. "Are you ready, Ari?"

"More than ready."

"Good, let's eat. I would like to ask the Lord's blessing over our food."

Ari nodded.

"Lord, we ask You for Your blessing over this food, and we give You thanks. We ask for Your blessing over Ari and Benjamin as they start their journey tomorrow. We cannot foresee any dangers along their way, but You can. Make their hearts sensitive to Your leading and Your will. Keep them safe and out of harm's way. May this journey give You glory. In Your name, we pray. Amen."

"Amen," Ari said in agreement.

After eating, Ari showed Klaus the twins' old room. "You can put your clothes in here. We can take one of the beds out to make more space."

"I'll wait until you return to do that," Klaus replied heading for the side door. "Right now, I'll put the horses up so you can get ready."

Ari graciously accepted and placed his writing utensils and Bible on the table. The ink needed time to dry so he set the paper next to his banner. *Time to pack*, he thought. He scanned the larder and collected some food and cooking equipment, and then he gathered bedding and extra clothes. Exhaustion settled in, and Ari could hardly keep his eyes open. "Time for bed."

A faint light glowed in the window against the dark sky and guided Benjamin the rest of the way to Ari's house. Both brothers bid each other farewell. "Klaus, I'm proud of you. You're a remarkable young man."

"Thank you, Benjamin. I'll be praying for both of you."

Ari grabbed Klaus' hand and thanked him again, "Without you, this journey would not be possible." Ari placed some money in Klaus' hand. "These are yours to keep for your work. If you need to replace anything for the farm, I'll reimburse you when I get back. I'll take good care of your brother." Klaus nodded.

After Ari paid Benjamin his wages, the two travelers headed south. The anticipation of seeing Magnus and Ivar created a sparkle in Ari's eyes. "I'm coming," he muttered.

Chapter 6

Higher Learning

Rays of morning light streamed through the window, captivating Tea's attention and rendering her oblivious to her parents' entrance. "Good morning," her mother greeted. Tea jumped. "I didn't mean to startle you."

Albert scanned the room looking for his godson. "Is Johann coming?" he asked.

"He said he wasn't hungry and that he'll be in the library," Tea replied.

"We'll save some food in case he needs it later," Maria offered.

Albert grasped the back of his chair and stood quietly in deep thought as he watched the steam ascending from their plates. He sat down and bowed his head. "Heavenly Father, we lift this food up to You and give You thanks and ask You to bless it. We know you always provide. We ask for your provision for Christana and all its people. In Your name, we pray. Amen."

Albert quietly expanded the prayer to himself. *And, Lord, show me how to help Johann during his father's absence. He must be concerned. Some kind of diversion would be helpful.* At that moment, he heard the church's organ. *Music, excellent idea! Thank you, Lord.*

After the servants picked up the empty dishes, Albert faced Maria and winked. Taking the hint, she excused herself and went to the garden for a walk.

Albert and Tea strolled down the hall. "Tea, has Johann watched you play the harpsichord?"

"No, Papa. I haven't played since Johann arrived."

"Perhaps, he would like to learn. Could you teach him?"

"Yes, I'd love to share my music with him. I'll look for my beginner's pieces Reverend Gudmund used with me."

"Splendid. Share with him at the midday meal. I'm going to see him now."

Johann had a disadvantage King Albert needed to rectify. The young man had very little formal education. Entering the library, Albert watched Johann stare aimlessly at the books on the shelves. His downcast face spoke volumes.

"Good morning, Johann."

Startled by the unexpected voice, Johann jumped. Turning toward Albert he grinned. Albert walked to Johann's side. "We have many books. What type of books interest you the most?"

"Books about the world. The Bible describes some countries, but not all. Those countries were from a long time ago, and they keep changing. I'm reading about a man named Christopher Columbus and his sailing discoveries. He was so brave."

"Yes, he was. He had the same thing you have: faith. Faith gives you strength. Would you like to learn more about the other countries and their people?"

"Yes, I would. I heard the organ this morning, and it reminded me of the church. I would like to learn more about the Bible. Magnus and Ivar will return with so much knowledge. I want to learn, too."

"Johann, I know some tutors who are knowledgeable in these subjects. I'll arrange for you to meet them so you can choose who you think will best help you. Reverend Lars is the best tutor for the Bible. He was one of the professors of the University where your brothers will attend."

"Thank you, Albert. I pray I'll always be as thoughtful as you are. For some reason, I feel hungry now."

"Maria thought you would be and had some food saved for you. Let's go get it." Albert put his arm around Johann's shoulder, and they walked together to the dining hall.

During the midday meal, Johann spent more time moving his food around the plate than putting it in his mouth. Tea took the opportunity and started humming a tune.

Johann tilted his head in her direction. "I like that song. I heard it many times when I was little. You played it on the harpsichord at Grandma's cottage."

"Yes, it's my favorite, too. Would you like to learn it?" Tea asked as she winked at her parents when Johann wasn't looking. Albert and Maria smiled at each other and excused themselves.

For the remainder of the afternoon, Johann practiced on the harpsichord with Tea. She watched Johann make many mistakes. *Is he doing this because he lacks talent for music, or is he making so many mistakes because he wants to sit by my side all afternoon?*

Albert and Maria took a long walk in the garden and checked on the dismantling of the glass hill. The sounds of nature soothed their aching ears. Upon nearing the entrance to the corral, the sentries opened the gated doors. The glass had been completely removed, and only a few wooden planks of the artificial hill remained. After the removal of the glass, the horses had been allowed to roam the pasture. Some of them kicked up their heels as they frolicked in the field. Others ran near the walled perimeter.

The special horses that could climb the hill of glass remained in their stalls. The Edelrosses' turn to roam around would be later in the afternoon after the other horses were returned to their stalls. One at a time, the special horses would be taken out of the corral and put through their paces by their trainer, Gunther.

Albert had met Gunther during the time he lived in Herrgott as a young boy. Gunther, an orphan, was several years younger than Albert. When his parents had died, Gunter's uncle had taken care of him and taught him how to take care of the king's horses. He demonstrated great promise over the years and progressed to training the Edelrosses.

During their youth, Albert and Gunther rode horses together. Occasionally, they would race each other. Most of the time, Albert would let Gunther win.

When Albert returned to Christana, Gunther came along as well, serving as one of the coachmen. Gunther stayed a few years but longed to return home. Albert gave him his blessings to return and a monetary gift for his service. When Albert had devised the contest, he sent a request to the king of Herrgott for the special horses. Gunther came with them. His demeanor had changed, and the trainer's face now bore a scar from his cheekbone to the corner of his mouth. No one knew what had happened, and no one asked.

The royal couple looked into the stable. Gunther greeted them, "Would you like to ride today, Sire?"

"Not today, Gunther," Albert replied. "Is there anything I can do for you? You must be missing Herrgott by now."

"You are kind to think of me, Sire," Gunther replied bowing his head. "My needs have been fulfilled in coming here and taking care of these horses."

"Gunther," Maria offered, "we want to make your stay with us as pleasing as possible. Come to us if you need anything."

Gunther marveled at the kindness offered to him. He unconsciously rubbed the scar on his face. Quickly, he dropped hand and bowed his head. "Thank you, Queen Maria."

Neither Albert nor Maria discussed the situation, but Albert sensed something odd. An uneasy feeling arose when he was around Gunther. *How could this be? I have known Gunther for many years. Maria knows him, too.* Albert kept a watchful eye on Gunther, while keeping his thoughts to himself.

Chapter 7

Heading South

A ri turned his head for one last look. Towering trees and thick brush blocked the remaining view of Christana. Thoughts of how he mistreated his twin sons before they had left, hounded him. Remorse gnawed at his inner being, stifling any desire to eat before his journey began. Seeking comfort, he laid his hand over his heart and felt the locket Johann had given him.

The Lord provides, Ari mouthed to himself. A smile appeared on his face. Benjamin noticed.

"Have you been this far south before?" Benjamin asked.

"My sons and I have traveled in every direction from Christana, but we never went as far as where we are headed. I have very little knowledge of this region. It will be an adventure for the both of us. We will cross a river in three days. Then, it will be another three days journey to Herrgott."

"The people of this region speak a language different from ours. I have learned some words from the carpenter, Hans. Maybe, it will be enough to help us get around."

"I'm thankful you're here, Benjamin. If I may ask, why did you give up your work with Hans?"

"Because of my father. His job as a lumberman was difficult. Swinging the axe to chop down trees was wearing his body down. He always knew how to use woodworking tools, and he made all our furniture and wooden objects. Papa taught me woodworking skills. That's why I began working for the carpenter to support my family. It's a worthy occupation, but it's not my aspiration."

Benjamin paused and looked at Ari, "Working with horses is my desire. It's Klaus' desire, too. When the opportunity to work for you came open, I gave my position with the carpenter to my father. It is easier work for him, and it's much closer to home than the forest."

"That makes sense. You're a thoughtful son. I'm blessed to have you with me."

The two traveled many miles before they lodged for the night. Looking at the moon peeking out from behind the clouds, Ari wondered if all his sons were observing it, too.

Hard compacted dirt along the river comprised the trail that guided the travelers. After riding for two more days, they found the ferry. The man in charge sat next to a boy of fifteen or more years of age. Ari noticed fresh scratches on the man's face and hands. Blood had dried and formed scabs. Nearby, a horse nibbled grass. Ari and Benjamin came closer and the older man stood up and greeted them.

Ari couldn't understand the language, but Benjamin could figure out a few of the words.

"Hello," Benjamin started, smiling and waving his hand. Pointing to himself, he said, "Benjamin."

Smiling, the old man did likewise. "Gustav." Then, he pointed to the boy. "Rolf."

Benjamin pointed to his traveling companion. "Ari."

Gustav nodded and offered his hand in friendship. Guessing correctly that these two wanted transport on his ferry, he pointed to his sign posted in three languages with the required fee. Ari paid.

Rolf secured a rope to a strap around his horse's midsection, untied the reins, and led the horse up the riverbank a short distance to compensate for the river's current. Ari and Benjamin watched the boy take the horse across the river. Actually, the horse swam, and the boy held onto the rope. Once he arrived on the other side, Rolf inserted the end of the rope into a pulley which was fastened to a tree across the river.

Then, he wrapped the end of the rope around the tree to secure it and waved to his father.

Ari turned to Benjamin. "Ask Gustav if he has seen Magnus and Ivar."

Gustav's eyes lit up, and he began talking as fast as he could. Benjamin couldn't understand a word he said. Finally, Gustav settled down and talked slowly. He pointed to Ari and asked, "Papa? Magnus, Ivar, Papa?"

It didn't take a translator to understand those words. Ari nodded and pointed to himself. "Papa of Magnus and Ivar."

Gustav jumped up and down. Benjamin and Ari stared at each other with the most puzzled look. Finally, Gustav settled down again and tried to explain what happened.

"Falke," he began, putting his thumbs side by side and flapping his fingers pronouncing the name as FAHL ku. Then, he started to claw at his face. "Falke," he repeated.

"That's how his face got scratched," Ari said aloud.

Trying to explain, Gustav fell carefully on his arm. When he stood up, he started to yell in pain and cradle his arm. Afterward, he said, "Magnus, Ivar." Ari's and Benjamin's puzzled faces swung back and forth. The old man smiled determined to tell them what had occurred.

Gustav laid his hand on his shoulder and started to moan loudly. Next, he pointed to Benjamin and said, "Magnus." He pointed to Ari, "Ivar." Grinning broadly, he pointed to himself, "Gustav." Then, he put Benjamin's hands together as if he was praying. He put Ari's hands grasping his hand. Next, he said "falke, falke," and pretended the bird was attacking by moving his free hand around his face. Gustav fell backward and imitated a popping noise. He reached for his shoulder and smiled. He looked up to the sky, folded his hands in prayer, and repeated, "Gut Gott gut Gott." *Good God, good God.*

Gustav's words and actions didn't need a translation now. A bird had attacked him, and Magnus and Ivar had prayed for him. When the bird returned, Gustav fell backward. Since Ivar still clenched his hand, his arm was pulled back in place.

Ari knew exactly how this could happen. He had prepared many animals for his family's food. He had noticed how joints in the shoulder and hip could move in and out of their sockets. This is what happened to Gustav's shoulder, and he gave the glory to God for the miracle. Gustav placed the money back in Ari's hand. Ari protested, but Gustav backed away shaking his head.

Gustav loaded his guests and their horses on his ferry. It looked like a flatbed boat. Holding onto a long pole, he pushed the ferry away from the shore, and the ferry drifted in the water. As the river current started to carry the ferry downstream, the boy pulled the end of the rope through the pulley, preventing its drift.

Once on the other side, Gustav told his son about the two guests on their ferry. Rolf's eyes lit up and immediately offered his hand. Gustav kept saying thank you, a phrase Benjamin could easily translate. Gustav and his son watched and waved at the two travelers until they were out of sight.

There it is again. Ari thought he saw movement on the other side of the river. His eyes scrutinized the landscape. *It could be an animal, it could be the wind, or is it something else?* He kept his suspicions from Benjamin as he didn't want to concern him. *This is Benjamin's first journey from home, and he should enjoy it.*

After they set up camp, Benjamin asked, "Do you get the feeling we're being followed?"

Ari tried to conceal his stunned look by momentarily turning his head. "It's probably a deer or another animal." The corner of Benjamin's mouth quirked in obvious skepticism.

During the evening meal, Benjamin slowly chewed his food. His eyes watched the glow of the campfire start to dwindle. "Ari, I'll stay up while you sleep."

"Actually, that's a good idea. Wake me up when you get too tired."

A few hours later, Benjamin had everything packed and woke Ari up.

"Let's move on in the cover of the darkness," Benjamin whispered. Ari quietly nodded and mounted his horse. Riding many miles in the moonless night, they missed seeing the looming structure on the other side of the river.

Much later, the sun warmed the sky with its morning colors. Benjamin fought to keep his eyes open. "Let's stop and eat," Ari said.

"Thank you," Benjamin replied. He slid off his horse and unpacked something to eat.

The bread had hardened and required water to make it edible. The dried meat provided great exercise for the jaw. Both travelers worked at eating their food but stopped upon hearing the approach of a horse. They stood up and turned their heads, searching. Their eyes were glued to the path. A finely dressed man on a horse as black as night came riding by. The sunlight reflected off the contours of his shoulder length, raven black hair giving it an eerie shade of deep blue. His sinister dark eyes glared at the two men still holding their food. "Good morning," the man said in their native language.

Ari cocked his head. *How did this man know what language we speak?* he wondered. "Good morning," Ari replied.

Perhaps his accent caused the man to say, "You're obviously not from around here, are you?"

Ari knew he had to be careful with his answer. "No," he replied. "I'm going to see my sons."

The man seized the opportunity to probe further, "What are the names of your sons?"

"Magnus and Ivar."

"What are your names?" the man persisted in his questions.

"I am Ari. This is Benjamin," Ari complied. Then, he started asking questions. "What is your name?"

The man tilted his head, gave a look of amazement, and answered the question. "I am Falke." He pronounced the name as FAHL ku. Looking down at his targets, he continued. "I enjoy an early morning ride. Do you?"

"Yes," answered Ari now wanting to keep his replies short and avoid more questions.

Then, the man turned to Benjamin and asked, "Do you enjoy early morning rides?"

Cold chills ran down Ari's spine. The hair on his arms stood straight up. Fortunately, his shirt had long sleeves so no one could see it. A queasy feeling swirled in his gut. He looked at Benjamin, who looked up at the man on the horse straight in the eye and firmly answered, "Yes, I do."

Falke gave an odd whistle and raised the hand not holding the reins. A thick leather glove completely covered that hand. All of a sudden, something swooped over Ari's head. A hawk landed on the gloved hand and began to eat the morsel of meat lodged in the palm of the glove. Ari marveled that the horse never flinched when the hawk flew near it. He had been trained to the bird.

After steadying the bird on his hand, Falke turned to Ari and Benjamin, "Safe journey, Benjamin. Safe journey, Ari, father of Magnus and Ivar."

Both Ari and Benjamin nodded goodbye to Falke. Falke gave a snide grin, guiding his horse on the path going north and whispered, "And father of Johann."

Quickly, Benjamin and Ari gathered their things, mounted their horses, and continued to head south. Neither spoke for several hours, quickening their pace.

Long shadows from the trees signaled the end of the day and they stopped. Ari couldn't hold it inside any longer. "How did you keep your composure with Falke?"

"I prayed," Benjamin replied. "The whole time I was keeping watch, I felt the urge to get up and leave our campsite. That's why I packed up. When he appeared, it confirmed my gut feeling. I knew the Lord was with us. So, I started using the promises of God for protection. That man is not of God. Could you feel it, too?"

"Yes, I felt an odd feeling in my gut."

"Good! That's Holy Spirit communicating with you."

"I feel like you are my elder taking care of me, instead of me taking care of you," Ari admitted.

"In a way, I am, Ari. I have walked with the Lord since I was a young boy. My parents read the Bible to me every day. I had to memorize scripture all the time. As a child, I didn't see the necessity for it. As I got older, I realize we have an enemy, and the Word of God is our weapon. After that, memorizing scripture became very easy. I'll share some with you if you like."

"Please, I need all the help I can get. Your son, Josef, is fortunate to have you for a father," Ari replied pronouncing the boy's name as YO-sef.

"Thank you, Ari. Children are a blessing, a gift from God. I try my best to be like our Heavenly Father. Let's finish up. I'll let you have first watch. I'm a little tired."

Ari kept a careful eye out, but he felt at ease. *Since Falke headed north, maybe we're out of harm's way,* he thought as he retrieved his banner with the cross and secured it to his saddle. Then, he reached for his heart and remembered the moment Johann gave him the locket.

He waited several hours before waking Benjamin. When Benjamin woke, he rubbed his eyes and tried to put his mind in focus. "Where am I?" He shook his head and finally remembered. Ari laid down and immediately fell asleep.

Chapter 8

Herrgott

Benjamin heard it first, a clip-clopping sound of approaching horses that broke the morning silence. Ari and Benjamin traded apprehensive glances. The approaching riders smiled and gave customary nods that calmed the travelers' fears. Doing his best to ask about Herrgott, Benjamin learned they could be there within an hour.

To their surprise, a bridge spanned the river and only required two copper coins per person for passage. Ari gladly paid the toll. The bridge opened up to a bustling city filled with pedestrians, riders, and an occasional carriage navigating the cobble stone streets. Ari's and Benjamin's style of clothing differed from the locals and periodically generated curious glances.

Ari searched for a tall structure. Finding the palace, he and Benjamin approached the front entrance, noting the two guards standing near the large doors. They dismounted and proceeded to carry out their mission. Immediately, both guards crossed their pikes, and the taller guard ordered, "Halt!"

Slowly, Ari removed the letter from his shirt and offered it to the guard who noticed the wax seal and shook his head. Turning around, he yelled something to the sentry that stood on the rampart of the palace wall. Very quickly, a servant walked out of the palace. When the guards placed their pikes in the upright position, the servant advanced and took the letter.

The tall guard smiled and winked at Ari. Ari took a deep breath and bowed his head. Both guards resumed their stance and stood solid as statues with their pikes in the upright position.

Benjamin scanned the buildings lining the street. "Let's find an inn and get something to eat before we look for Magnus and Ivar."

"I'm glad I have a tour guide with me," Ari teased.

Benjamin spotted a carved sign portraying images of food. His limited vocabulary included the necessary words to read the sign. After securing their horses on the rail, they entered the inn. The noise of patrons enjoying a midday meal filled the room. Finding an empty table, the weary travelers sat down.

Ari looked around to see what the other diners were eating. He saw something that looked and smelled delicious. When the innkeeper came over, Ari pointed to a nearby plate of food, pointed to himself, and raised one finger. The man smiled and nodded. Benjamin raised two fingers indicating to bring them two of the same food. The man smiled and nodded again.

The innkeeper dipped his ladle into the pots of prepared food and returned with their order. He set Ari's plate on the table in front of him. Then, he set Benjamin's two plates of food in front of him and left. Benjamin's mouth dropped open, his eyes staring at the twin plates. Ari grabbed his midsection and laughed outrageously. The other patrons looked at the two, looked at their table, and joined in the laughter. They raised their mugs in the air and returned to their own food.

Ari lifted his spoon and paused in midair. Someone had entered the inn and yelled, "Papa!"

All the men turned to look at the man in the doorway, but only one man stood up. "Magnus!" Ari yelled.

Quickly, Magnus raced to his father, and they both hugged each other's neck. "Magnus, I'm so sorry. I asked the Lord to help me, and He did. Magnus," Ari paused inhaling deeply, "Johann and I are reunited. I came to see you and Ivar as fast I as could." Ari stepped back and looked into his son's eyes and pleaded, "Please forgive me for the terrible things I said to you."

Magnus sat down and motioned for his father to do the

same. "Papa, if you hadn't said those words, Ivar and I wouldn't be here. It may sound strange, but God moved on that situation and made something wonderful out of it. Ivar and I forgave you before we left Christana. We prayed for God's will to flow in your life. I can see He answered our prayer."

"Thank you, Son. How did you know I was in here?"

"I saw a banner fluttering in the breeze. It grabbed my attention. When I got closer, I recognized your horse and saddle."

"Where's Ivar?"

"He's at the University helping with the meals. I didn't have to help, so I took a walk. He's going to be so happy when he hears you're here." Then Magnus looked at the extra plate.

"Please, join us," Benjamin offered, pushing the plate over to Magus who immediately began to eat.

"Who's at our farm?" Magnus asked.

Benjamin answered, "My brother, Klaus. We're learning the trade."

"That's another answer to prayer. Did you use the ferry?" Magnus asked.

"Yes, we did," Ari said. "Gustav shared with us how you two prayed with him, and how his injured arm was fixed."

"How did you understand what he was saying?"

"That's a long story. I'll save it for later." Ari smiled at the thought of Gustav. "Did you see any strange birds on your journey?"

"No, we saw very few birds riding here. Probably predator birds flying around." Magnus returned his attention to his plate of food. Ari and Benjamin looked at each other and remained quiet.

"How do you participate in the classes at the University? Ari asked. "You don't speak Herrgott."

"We have a bilingual teacher to help us. Our first class is learning the language. We're receiving lessons about the Bible, but only in our language at the moment. They want to make sure we understand what's being taught. Papa, the teachers say our reading skills are very good, but our number skills need some work." Magnus grinned. Ari gave a little chuckle.

Magnus paused and turned his ear toward the sound of a tolling bell. "That's Vespers, our call for prayer. Ivar will be there. Papa, I'll ask if we can have our evening meal here tonight."

Ari stood up and handed him Johann's letter. As Magnus walked out, the tall guard from the palace walked in. He glanced around the room. Finding Ari and Benjamin, he walked over to their table. Pointing to Ari, the guard motioned for him to follow. Benjamin started to get up, but the guard held out his hand and shook his head. Then, the guard smiled and winked. Benjamin took a deep breath and sighed. He surmised this was a friendly invitation. Ari left money on the table and told Benjamin to wait for him.

Thoughts of why he was being summoned rumbled through his mind. Ari followed the escorting guard all the way inside the palace courtyard to a tranquil garden. A finely dressed man sat on a bench waiting for him. The guard bowed to the sitting man and left.

"Good day to you, Ari," the man spoke in Ari's language. "You don't know me. I have the honor to be the king of Herrgott, I am Stefan. Now I have the honor of meeting you." Stefan slightly bowed his head. The sunlight reflected off his neatly trimmed winter-white hair and beard. Wrinkles framed the corners of his aging eyes. The weight of his position dug deep furrows in between his eyebrows. He kept an inquiring eye on Ari perhaps assessing the man's character.

"It's an honor to meet you, King Stefan." Ari replied.

Quickly, King Stefan raised his hand and interrupted him. "Relatives do not use the word king." Ari had the most puzzled look on his face. The king grinned. "You don't know the contents of the letter, do you?"

"No, King St—" Ari started to say.

"Ari," Stefan interrupted again, "when Tea and Johann have a child, it will be your grandchild and my great-grandchild. Maria is my daughter. Family uses family names."

"May I sit down?" Ari humbly asked.

"Forgive me, please do."

Ari's heart pounded as he grasped the situation—another king being kind to him!

"You have traveled very far to come to Herrgott. I understand your other sons are here studying at the University. Did you encounter any problems along the way?"

Ari lowered his eyes then looked at Stefan. He told the king everything about his meeting with Gustav and Falke.

Stefan listened intently and then placed a hand to his chin letting it trail to the end of his beard. His eyes momentarily drifted sideways while assessing the information. "Thank you for your honesty and coming to meet with me."

"Thank you for your kindness. If there is anything I can do for you or your kingdom, I'll do my best to fulfill this pledge."

Stefan smiled. "Thank you, Ari. There is one thing. You'll see my granddaughter, Tea, more than I will. Share my love with her."

Ari stood up and bowed to King Stefan. The old king did not object to the gesture. He remained seated and nodded to Ari.

As Ari straightened up, King Stefan asked, "When are you leaving?"

"If I see both of my sons tonight, I'll leave at sunrise tomorrow. I need to return to my farm."

"At first light, please come to the palace."

"I will," Ari replied.

"Ari, any time you return to Herrgott, you are always welcome in my home."

"I would be honored to come." With one last quick nod, Ari left.

Stefan watched Ari walk out of sight, then he called for his servant and gave an order. The servant made haste to carry out the command.

The inn door opened and Ari looked up. The corner of his mouth drew up in a pucker. *Wrong guy. Maybe the next one.* The door opened again. This time Ivar raced through the doorway in search of his father. Ari extended his arms wide and gave him a long embrace. Placing his twin sons side by side, Ari stepped back to admire Magnus and Ivar in their ministerial attire. A glow of serenity presided on his sons' faces. Ari took a deep breath and continued to relish the moment, for he knew it would be a long time—perhaps months—before he would visit them again.

After their meal, the bonging bell announced the time for vespers. Magnus pulled a letter out of his pocket. "This is for Johann."

"Goodbye, Papa," the twins said in unison.

"Goodbye, sons. I don't know when, but I will return." Ari watched his sons walk through the doorway and into the night.

At first light, Ari and Benjamin packed their saddle bags. Heading for the palace, Ari thought about the location where Falke had appeared. That queasy feeling in his gut came back.

The Word, Ari told himself as he touched the locket under his shirt. *I'll meditate on the Word of God.* "**Call upon Me in your day of trouble, and I will deliver you,**" he quoted to himself. "This qualifies as a day of trouble," Ari muttered.

Approaching the palace, they noticed a group of guards on horseback. At first glance, Ari counted ten or more men. Several canvas-covered wagons waited nearby. The tall guard joined the group. He smiled, but he did not wink this time. The other guards watched his every move. In his best words of Christana's language, he said, "We go north. Go together. Is okay?"

Ari stared at the guard repeating his words, "Is okay." He quickly assessed the situation. *There's safety in numbers. Thank you, Lord. You provide.*

Benjamin quietly exhaled. He closed his eyes momentarily as an expression of relief spread across his face. *I hope they're traveling all the way to the ferry, Lord.*

The tall guard, who was the captain of the group, gave the command and his group progressed toward the bridge. The toll keeper stood to the side allowing them to pass. In the rear, draft horses strained against their harnesses as they pulled the laden wagons keeping an even pace.

Travel time seems to go faster, Benjamin thought. *Maybe it's because we don't have to be on guard. We have plenty of guards with us.* Benjamin occasionally scanned the woods just as a precaution.

The sun touched the treetops announcing the end of the day. Each guard attended to their duties of setting up camp and taking care of the horses. Ari spoke to the guards making hand motions for stirring a bowl, "Kochen." Pointing to himself, he made a sour face, "Mau." Pointing to Benjamin and himself, then the horses, Ari smiled and nodded. "Ross, gut."

The tall guard pointed to the horses and nodded. The other guards rolled their eyes shaking their heads. Ari couldn't tell for sure, but he thought he was the subject of a few jokes that night.

Midway to the ferry, the captain pointed his finger toward the opposite side of the river. Another river joined the Herrgott River. The guard pointed again to the north side of the adjoining river. An ominous castle loomed near the river's edge. Mounted on a tower, a hawk-emblemed banner waved in the wind. Cold chills ran down Ari's spine. *We missed this.*

Benjamin squinted and sneered at the banner. "No weapon formed against me will prosper," he said aloud.

A memorized verse, Ari surmised. *I'll find out what book it's located in.*

The fading sunlight prompted the guards to make camp for the night. They detected no visible signs of anyone or anything following the group. Early the next day, the group reached the ferry.

Gustav recognized the colors and banners of the guards. Quickly, he sent Rolf and his horse with the rope to the guards' side of the river.

Waiting for the boy, the captain motioned for three guards to bring their horses forward and stand next to him. Those three went over first. Ari, Benjamin, and the tall guard took the next ferry ride. After they boarded, the captain of the guard handed Ari a letter. Ari noted a wax seal on it that was different from the original letter he had first carried. Ari perceived its importance and tucked it away in his shirt. Neither man uttered a word.

On the other side of the river, Ari and Benjamin extended their hands in friendship to the captain. "Danke," the travelers said. The tall guard smiled and winked one last time.

While they shook hands, Ari noticed two of the guards' horses had their saddles removed. The tall guard reached for the reins and handed them to Ari and spoke two words, "King Albert."

Maybe these mares are a gift for Stefan's daughter or granddaughter, Ari thought as he admired the sleek lines of each horse. He smiled at the tall guard and nodded.

Chapter 9

School Begins

H e stretched his fingers hoping to relieve the cramping ache. "This is hard," Johann complained sitting at the harpsicord. "I try to curve my fingers and put them on the keys, but they're not cooperating. When I want them to reach for another key, they start twitching and will not go."

"Johann, my dear, it takes time," Tea said encouragingly.

"I can read any kind of book, but it's difficult to read music," Johann bemoaned and pursed his lips.

Placing her hands on her hips, Tea narrowed her eyebrows. "Stop your whining. If little children can learn, so can you, but it takes a desire to learn and lots of practice."

"I'm sorry," Johann apologized. "If I was a child, I would love to have you as my teacher."

"I am your teacher, and you are acting like a child."

"Tea, you'd be a wonderful teacher of children. Your mother taught me to read when I lived here. My grandmother continued the lessons when we returned to her cottage. I was fortunate to have reading instruction. Some of the children in Christana do not have parents who can read. They need an opportunity to learn, too."

"Johann, you're thinking like a sovereign. You're envisioning the peoples' needs. Maybe Mama would like to teach again."

Maria walked by in the hallway. Her ears perked up at the mention of her name, and she entered the room. "Hello, you two. What would I like to teach?" she asked.

"Teach the children of Christana how to read, Mama!"

"That's a great idea, Tea. We need to talk with your father."

Albert's ears caught his name as he passed by and came inside. "What are my ladies up to this morning?"

"Tea is thinking of teaching the children of Christana to read if they don't know how," Maria said.

"Tea," Albert said puffing his chest out, "you're thinking like a sovereign."

"Papa," Tea interrupted, "it was Johann's idea."

Albert looked at Johann with great admiration. "The Lord picked a good one for my daughter. We need to approach this with wisdom. Let's devise a plan before we announce our intentions. Tea, your beginner books and papers are in the library. Ladies, perhaps you can use them in your instructions."

Albert walked over to Johann and put his arm around the young man's shoulder. "My sovereign-in-training and I are going to confer with the counselors. Christana's children will have an opportunity to learn. Johann, the last time I called the Court Counselors together was to find a method for selecting suitors for Tea. Maria helped me find the solution. This will be an easier process to develop. Our counselors are well educated. This is an asset we can use."

Albert's servant found the counselors in the accounting

room. Each one had a position in the organizational procedures of the palace. Their responsibilities included the financial affairs of the town of Christana and of the entire kingdom. They stopped their work and followed the servant. The Head Counselor stroked his gray beard as he walked, wondering what service he could do for the king or if the king simply needed their advice.

After the counselors settled in their chairs, they quietly waited for the king to talk. Albert looked at Johann and motioned for him to address the group. Johann gasped. He was supposed to simply observe, not talk! Johann fumbled for his locket, swallowing hard. It wasn't there. *Papa has it!* He'd forgotten. Looking from patient face to patient face, he didn't know what to do. *Lord, give me guidance!*

"Gentlemen," Johann began, "I admire your wisdom and knowledge. I want to learn from you and your experiences. Having you as counselors benefits our citizens of Christana."

The older men at the table smiled. This young man had acknowledged their ability to contribute to the kingdom. Albert smiled, too.

"Each one of you has had the privilege to read and learn about many subjects. As a young child, I was fortunate to learn to read. Some of our citizens do not know how to read. Therefore, they cannot teach their children this valuable skill and tool."

The smiles of counselors faded away, ashamed that they hadn't previously advised about this void in their kingdom. Finally, one of them asked, "What can we do to help?"

"If we had a place of learning, perhaps here at the palace, the children of Christana could learn to read and contribute more to our community."

The counselors leaned over and talked with one another. The oldest of the group responded, "Children who want to read should have the opportunity. Do you have someone for the instruction?"

"Yes," replied Johann. "I have two."

"Splendid," the counselor remarked. "Since most of the families would want their children in this new school, we need to have a way to assess which children need the most help. As the school progresses, maybe we could teach some other courses such as mathematics and science."

"Excellent!" Johann replied.

The counselors huddled again. Albert and Johann strained their ears to decipher their low murmurs. After a few minutes, both heard one word, "Agreed." The group straightened up in their chairs. Their smiles indicated a workable solution.

"Here's what we propose," said the Head Counselor. "Display parchments announcing the establishment of a reading school and the assessments for the children. Have the town criers make the proclamations, too. What are your thoughts for ages six through sixteen?"

Johann leaned over to Albert and quietly discussed the age group. It was a range that could be adjusted later if necessary. "Agreed," Johann replied.

The counselors started discussing the assessments and quickly came up with an idea. The youngest counselor proposed the plan. "We can have a table in front of the palace for the parents to register their children. Each of us can sit at different tables for the reading evaluation. The first table would be alphabet recognition, the next table would be sound recognition, and the next table would be word recognition. The final table would have scriptures from the Bible. If a child can read scriptures, his or her skills would be graded at the highest level."

Albert and Johann liked this suggestion and nodded.

"Each child will have their name on the paper along with their age," the counselor continued. "As the child progresses through the assessment, the evaluator will put the number of the successfully completed level. Once the child can no longer continue, the paper is kept, and the child is asked to return to their parents. The results will be announced the following day at the end of the church service. Hopefully, the classrooms are big enough for all the students. If necessary, the highest readers could help your teachers."

This time Albert spoke, "Gentlemen, this is a proud day for Christana. Our citizens are blessed to have you. Thank you. Complete your preparations. I'll let you know when the reading materials are ready to begin our first school."

The counselors bowed to the king and left all talking at the same time and sharing ideas. Albert turned to Johann. "I put you in the center of attention today on purpose. There will be situations where you'll have to make decisions very quickly. It's not easy to do when people are staring at you while you're thinking. You did well."

"Thank you, Albert," Johann said exhaling a big breath of air. "It was a little daunting, but when I focused on the goal, it became easier to address the counselors. The needs of the children were more important than mine.

Albert thought about the events of the day. *Johann is focused on his calling.* A smile spread across his face. "Let's go see how our teachers are doing."

Tea and Maria found the papers and books. They separated the materials in the order of difficulty.

"One day, Tea, you will have little ones of your own. You'll want to save their papers, too."

"And, you'll want them to give you a big hug," said her father entering the room. Tea immediately ran to her father and hugged his neck.

"I love you, Papa."

"I love you," Albert replied. "And I have good news. The counselors have a system to evaluate the reading levels for the children. When you're ready, we'll post the announcement."

"We're going to need the scribes to help copy these materials," Tea added.

"There will be too many pages to copy. It is time for Christana to get a printing press," Albert noted. "We need to move with the new inventions if we want to keep current with the world."

Chapter 10

Journey Home

Ari turned around for one last look of the ferry landing, but the bushes and trees joined together and blocked the view. His attention turned to the past few days. *Those guards, what are they for? The canvas-covered wagons, what's in them?*

The horse tethered to Benjamin's saddle swished her tail. Long hairs fanned out catching Ari's attention. *Gorgeous horse. I want to learn more. Perhaps, Johann could tell me.*

Twilight snuck up on them, and they stopped to camp. The sun dipped under the horizon, and darkness spread quickly. Even though they were far from the ferry, Ari and Benjamin were on same side of the river as the castle. Ari stayed up first. He strained his ears to pick up any unusual noise while he scanned the woods for movement. All was quiet except for the horses occasionally snorting while they rested. Midway through the night, he woke up his replacement.

The rising sun stretched its rays over Benjamin while he prepared the morning meal. The nutty aroma of bubbling porridge drifted toward Ari and ended his few hours of rest. "Good morning, Benjamin. One more day and we'll be home."

"Getting tired of my cooking?" Benjamin quipped.

"You're better than me any day of the week."

Around the bend, Ari spotted a familiar fork in the path. "There it is!" he shouted. "There's the path to our home."

Benjamin envisioned his family and beamed. *Almost home!*

Ari envisioned Falke's intimidating encounter, and his gut

turned queasy. *Is this one of Your warning signs, Lord?* he silently prayed. *Should we be careful sharing this experience?* Ari remained quiet during his meditation.

"Ari, are you in deep thought?" Benjamin asked.

"Uh, yes." Ari hesitated, not knowing what to say. "I'm troubled about our meeting with Falke. Should we repeat it?"

"I'm not telling my wife. I don't want to worry her in case we travel that path again. That man seems like a tormentor. I pray I'll never see him again."

"I'm perplexed about those guards and their covered wagons. What was their mission?"

"Perhaps King Albert will know," Benjamin said.

"Perhaps." Ari narrowed his eyes, spotting the town square in the distance and motioned with his hand. "Your trip is finished. Go." Benjamin's eyes sparkled. He handed over the mare's reins and pointed his horse toward his home. Ari watched him go, rubbing the small of his back trying to soothe his aching spine. "Just a little bit more and I can go home, too," he muttered.

Pulling the two mares behind him, he approached the palace guards. "These are for King Albert." One guard nodded and allowed to Ari enter. The other guard came forward and took the horses.

Recognizing Ari, an older servant came forward and escorted him to Johann. Ari stopped in the doorway to watch his son as he sat near the window. Johann looked up. He leaped from his chair and ran toward his father. "Papa, you're home."

Ari gathered his son in his arms. *Thank You, Lord.* He savored the moment before he dropped his arms and stepped back. "I have a letter for Albert," he said, pulling it from his shirt.

"He'll be here in a few minutes. He has been working with the counselors."

Ari reached in his shirt again. "I have a letter for you from your brothers."

Johann's eyes lit up, and he took the letter. He recognized

the handwriting. Ivar had a familiar style with the letter J.

While Johann read his letter, Tea walked in. "Good to see you, Ari. I hope your journey was safe but exciting."

"It was exciting, and we were safe," Ari said patting the locket over his heart. "The Lord provided." Ari looked at the table full of stacked papers. "You two are very busy. Are you making books?"

Johann looked up from reading his letter. "Papa, we're starting reading lessons for the children who need help. Tea and Maria will be the teachers. As soon as we have the materials ready, we can begin."

"Is there an age limit? May I come?" Ari teased.

"I asked the same question, Ari," Albert said as he walked in. "I'm currently on the waiting list." Everyone chuckled.

Ari handed Albert the letter, but he put it aside to read later. "I understand you came back with some extra horses. Were there any problems on your journey?" Albert asked.

"No," replied Ari. "Coming back, the Herrgott guards were with us until we reached the ferry. That's when we were given the two mares.

Hearing that there were guards with them, Albert stiffened ever so slightly. Then, he relaxed. "Ari, you must be hungry and tried, would you like to dine with us tonight?"

"Your invitation is most appreciated, but I want to get to my home and farm. Perhaps another time."

"There will be many more times, Ari."

Ari walked over to Tea and placed her hands in his hands. Everyone watched. Tea studied Ari's eyes. "Tea, Stefan sends his love. He wanted to be here personally to express it himself." Tears gathered in Tea's eyes. Ari tenderly hugged her. "This is from your grandfather."

"Thank you, Ari. This gesture warms my heart."

Albert walked Ari down the hall while Johann continued to read his letter. During the walk, Ari shared what happened on his journey. Albert reminded Ari about the responsibility concerning royal matters.

"That's why I was careful with my words. Benjamin will be discreet, too." Both men shook hands, and Ari departed.

Passing the church, Ari looked up at the sky. "Thank You, Lord. You provided for my safe journey. I lift my hands up to You. You are my banner. The victory belongs to You."

An observer cocked his eyebrow as he watched the man on his horse go by. "I disagree, Ari, father of Johann. Victory will belong to me," he quietly hissed. Adjusting his cloak, he ducked out of sight.

Trotting down the lane, exhaustion and hunger washed over Ari and his shoulders slumped. His sagging eyelids perked up when he saw Elina's cottage. "In a few years, my sons will be living here." He looked for his house, but the barn blocked his view. Rounding the corner, he saw smoke rising from the chimney that slowly disappeared in the sky. "I hope Klaus has enough for both of us."

Ari opened the side door. Klaus stiffened up. Recognizing Ari, he relaxed his body and exhaled deeply. "Welcome home, Ari. Good timing; the food is ready."

During their meal, Klaus' eyes sparkled as he listened, imagining everything Ari described. Ari noticed and continued, but he really wanted to hear about the progress of his farm.

Klaus quickly brushed through farm updates and ended with a different subject. "Ari, when can we begin saddle breaking the horses?"

"Tomorrow. It's time to share my technique."

"May I continue to stay here?" Klaus asked quietly.

"I'd love to have you stay. It gets lonely here. Will your parents agree with this?"

"Papu was the one who suggested it."

Ari rolled his eyes and enjoyed a comforting laugh. Klaus shared his boyish grin. "Ari, I'll cleanup for the night." Ari laid his hand on Klaus' shoulder as he walked by and went straight to bed never waking up until the morning light filtered through the window.

Chapter 11

Horse Sense

L ight filtered through the window, stretching over the bed and touching Ari's face. "I did it again!" He quickly got up and entered the cooking room. Benjamin and Klaus patiently waited for him at the table.

"Good morning Ari," both brothers said simultaneously. They sat upright on the bench with their arms resting on the table. Klaus had already shared with Benjamin that they would saddle break a horse today.

"Good morning," Ari replied. "Are you two prepared to learn the rest of my trade secrets of horse training?"

The brothers' eyes became bigger, their grins wider. Ari grinned, too, as he eyed the kettle hanging over the fire. "We'll get started as soon as I finish eating."

Klaus jumped up and poured Ari's porridge in a bowl and placed it on the table. *I'm enjoying the royal treatment I'm getting this morning, but will the brothers enjoy the treatment of their first lesson?* Ari wondered.

They all headed for the barn, but Ari stopped to look at the other animals. The chickens pecked at their morning grain and the horses quenched their thirst with fresh water in troughs. "The brothers got up very early today and started the chores," Ari muttered.

Benjamin and Klaus waited in the barn. When Ari entered, he saw Benjamin holding a saddle, and Klaus holding a blanket, bridle, and reins. He calmly walked over to Benjamin. Ari took the saddle and laid it on the nearby rail. He went to Klaus and retrieved the equipment and laid it next to the saddle. "Wait here."

Ari entered the tact room and returned with several leather straps and a rope tied to a long stick. Both brothers looked at each other with a puzzled look on their faces and shrugged. Ari laid the straps over his shoulder and walked up to Benjamin. Pointing his finger to the ground, and uttered, "Dop bu kem."

Benjamin pulled his head back and gave Ari an odd look. Ari pointed to the ground and uttered the same words again, "Dop bu kem."

Confusion flooded Benjamin's mind, and he wondered if Ari was having a mental issue, but he obediently stood there and said nothing. Ari grinned.

Suddenly and quite forcibly, Ari began tightening a leather strap around Benjamin's chest to the point of pain. Next, Ari tightened straps around his arms. When Benjamin started to move, Ari flipped the stick with the attached rope and struck the ground. Benjamin jumped. Ari tied one end of a larger rope to the strap around Benjamin's chest and secured the other end of the rope to the rail. Afterward, Ari commanded, "Dop bu kem."

Once Benjamin was tethered to the rail, Ari turned and walked over to Klaus. Klaus looked at Ari with wild eyes and began violently shaking his head back and forth.

Ari carefully placed the straps on the rail next to Klaus. He gently reached out and rubbed his arms. Klaus' whole body stiffened, and he flinched his arms. Ari very softly repeated the words, "Dop bu kem." Ari began to rub Klaus' back. Klaus began to relax his stiff muscles. Ari could feel it. Ari continued to use soft pats and rubs on both of Klaus' arms, back, and neck. Next, he picked up one strap and gently rubbed it on Klaus' arms and back. Klaus relaxed a little more. Occasionally, he would turn his head to see what Ari was doing. Finally, Ari gently placed one strap on Klaus' arm. Klaus stood there, fully relaxed, and watched Ari put the strap on. Klaus took a deep breath and rubbed his nose with his free arm.

Ari noticed, patted Klaus' arm, and gently said, "Palipa." Ari backed up a little and asked, "Do you two have any questions?"

Any questions? Benjamin thought. *He has to be kidding.* Not wanting to insult Ari's demonstration, Benjamin tried tactfully to address the situation. "Ari, your technique is unique, but I don't understand why you bound me with straps and tied me to the rail. I couldn't understand the gibberish you kept repeating."

Ari nodded, "And neither does the horse understand your language, or why you are binding and tying him or her up. Did you want to resist? Did you find it difficult to relax?"

"Yes," Benjamin replied. "I never relaxed."

"How was your experience, Klaus?" Ari asked looking at him.

"It felt strange, but it wasn't as scary as Benjamin's treatment. When I started to feel you were not going to hurt me, I could relax a little."

"I noticed," Ari confided. "That was the moment I stopped. When you took a deep breath and rubbed your nose, I knew you were relaxing. That means you're trusting what I was doing to you. Most importantly, you're showing me respect by allowing me to put straps on you without objection. You both have had your first lesson in saddle breaking today."

"That was a horse lesson?" Benjamin asked. "We didn't get near any horses."

Ari smiled, "The first lesson is training the people. The next lesson is working with the horse."

"Ari, I have a better perspective now," Klaus said. "Can we take the straps off now?"

"Sure, let me help you." Removing the straps from Benjamin, Ari shared these words of wisdom, "Horses are like people. They have attitudes, personalities, and feelings. We're the smarter of the two. God made us that way. It's important we take care of His animals. The horse is your friend. We take care of our friends, and they'll take care of us."

Benjamin took a deep breath, relieved to have the straps off. Ari looked at Klaus. "No teasing your brother about the straps and rope. I could have picked you first. One more important lesson to share," Ari continued. "Did you feel as though I was a bully?"

"Uh, yes," Benjamin said. "And I didn't like it."

"You can be a bully to a horse, but you do not get their total respect. They'll obey you in some commands, but they won't trust you in every situation. The same thing happens in life," Ari continued. "Bullies are looking for someone that will give in to their intimidations. We can learn from horses. Now, it's time for the outside training."

"And?" the voice rang out. Ari froze, the blood draining from his face as he looked around the barn.

"Ari, are you all right?" Benjamin asked.

"I thought I heard something."

This time it came as faint as a whisper. *And?* Guilt washed over Ari. Turning to face the two brothers, Ari knew what he had to do. He inhaled deeply and confessed. "I know what a bully is. I was one to my own sons."

Klaus start to speak, but Ari put his hands up. "If I do not admit my own sin, how can I help others? I'd be a hypocrite.

I've been many things is my life, but I don't want to be thought of as that."

A lightness flooded into Ari. It reminded him of the day the Lord healed his heart driving out the bitterness. He heard the faint whisper again. *Well done, my son.*

Benjamin walked over and laid his hand on Ari's shoulder. "We know, but hearing you say it is a witness to me. I'm not brave enough to expose my wrong doings, but I'll work on it. Thank you, Ari."

Ari nodded and gathered the straps. While in the tact room, he offered a prayer, "Thank you, Jesus. I praise Your holy name." He straightened his shirt up and joined the brothers. "There are three mares who need to be haltered and begin the training course. That's the next step in saddle breaking. I'll demonstrate the first stages of training with one of them. You two will work with the other two horses later. I'll need to be there with you while you are training the horses with these new skills—for your safety and theirs."

Benjamin and Klaus both chuckled. They put the saddle, blanket, and reins back in the storage room. Ari picked up a halter and proceeded to the corral. One of the targeted mares stood close by. Klaus put some grain in the bin and allowed her to enter the corral. Now, Ari had to gain the confidence and respect of the horse.

Benjamin and Klaus found a comfortable spot on the rail and watched. Ari ignored the horse. Every time the mare walked near him, Ari turned his back and walked away. Soon, the horse followed Ari everywhere. Ari winked at the brothers. "I think she likes me, but don't treat your ladies this way."

With a few well-planned maneuvers, Ari slipped the halter on the mare. The horse never protested. Ari rubbed both sides of her head and neck. "This is the beginning. There are many more skills to learn."

After inhaling their midday meal, Klaus and Benjamin hurried to the corral. While holding an imaginary halter and lead rope, Klaus mimicked the actions Ari had demonstrated earlier on how to put the halter on the unbroken horse. Benjamin nodded and headed toward his targeted horse. Their relationship was mutual. When he ignored the horse, the horse ignored him. Klaus silently prayed for his brother to have success.

Benjamin walked over to the rail next to Ari and handed the equipment to Klaus. "You try. I want to sit down."

Klaus muffled his chuckle and confidently took the halter and lead rope. He approached the uncooperative horse and made eye contact. The horse snorted. Then, Klaus walked away. Curious, the horse followed. Klaus repeated the action and achieved the same results. After a rubbing the leather straps on the horse's cheeks, Klaus went for the goal and placed the halter on.

"Why couldn't I do that, Ari?" Benjamin asked.

"It takes time. You're used to a horse that has already been trained. Those horses are used to us, but this is a whole new behavior for these horses to learn. Can they trust you? Klaus," Ari hollered, "take the halter off and give it to your brother." Ari looked at the dejected young man. "Try again, Benjamin."

Ari watched and grinned. Benjamin's body movements countered the horse's reactions, and the mare allowed the novice to place the halter on her face. Benjamin walked a little taller back to the rail.

Ari gave him a hardy pat on the back. "The horses we haltered today need to start the exercise arena. And it's time to saddle train the other haltered horses. I'll start with one while you two observe. Remember, I need to be with you while you're learning. Good results come from good procedures."

"Ari," Klaus began, "this is easy for you. Do you ever want an exciting challenge?"

Benjamin's body stiffened as he looked at Ari. Ari remained calm. "Klaus, every day I get up is a challenge. I do not take life for granted. Some days are wonderful, and some days can be scary."

"You get scared?" Klaus asked.

"Everyone is capable of being scared. The brave do not let that emotion hinder their actions. If they're afraid, they do it being afraid. The fear will pass. Let faith, not fear, control your life."

"Klaus, how would you like to go to the inn with me tonight for the evening meal?" Ari asked. "Would you like to go, Benjamin?"

"Yes!" said Klaus.

"Could we start early?" Benjamin asked. "I want to spend time with my son before he goes to sleep."

"That's a great idea. Finish work early," Ari said. "Let's introduce our new student to the obstacles in life in the arena."

Later in the day, the three horsemen arrived at the inn. The innkeeper teasingly asked, "Is it your turn to cook tonight, Ari? I haven't seen you for a long time."

"You have heard about my cooking skills," Ari replied as he patted the man on the back. Ari turned, pointed to the door and waved goodbye to Benjamin. He gladly followed the direction.

Chapter 12

The Letter

Finishing the last word in his letter, Albert leaned back in his chair still clutching the paper. His chest rose, and he emitted a deep sigh as lines of sorrow filled his face. "You and that hawk. Now you're hurting people. Why?" The grieved king knelt and prayed, "Lord, I need Your help. The problem is getting worse. I lift my hands up to You. You alone can give the victory. You are my banner. I know You will provide. Show the path we need to follow. Holy Spirit guide me. In Jesus' name, I pray. Amen."

Although the problem remained, calmness swirled inside of Albert like smoke filling a bottle. He handed the letter to Maria. Reading her father's greeting her face glowed, but her hands trembled as she read the rest.

She looked into Albert's eyes. "Will I ever be able to see my father again? Not only do I fear for his life, I fear for our lives, too."

"Maria, we need to be strong and trust in the Lord. We need to keep this information to ourselves for now. I'll talk to Johann. We'll let Tea know later. She's so busy with the planning for the new school. This will be too disturbing for her."

"I agree. I should go and work on my plans. School starts in less than two weeks."

Maria shuffled her papers around trying to disguise her feelings. Her somber face betrayed her efforts. Johann and Tea sensed a change, and Tea gave Johann that look of "do something."

Johann pondered for a moment then asked, "Maria, When the children are receiving lessons, how are they supposed to address you and Tea?"

Maria glanced up. "That thought never occur to me. Did it occur to you, Tea?"

"No, Mama. We should have a title to address us that shows respect, but maybe a little less formal during the time the children are in our care."

"Well said, my daughter. Let's compile a list and choose an appropriate title."

Johann walked over to Maria and bowed. "Your Loveliness." He stood up again and winked at her. Maria giggled. Johann turned to face Tea and winked at her.

My Johann, Tea thought giving him a grateful look. *You made Mama laugh.*

As the two teachers worked with the reading papers, Johann wrote down titles he had heard at the palace and said them aloud: "Queen, Princess, Your Royal Highness, Lady, Your Grace, Ma'am."

"Ma'am," Maria repeated lifting her head. "It shows respect without displaying too much formality. I like it."

"I do, too, Mama," Tea agreed. "It's a title that applies to both of us."

"Great," Johann said, and he circled the word Ma'am. "Now we need someone to greet the children as they come in each morning. Someone who can bless them and set the day in a positive mood. Please note, I'm not volunteering for the job."

"Johann, you'll be very busy. You're going to be studying, too, remember?" Tea giggled. "This sounds like a great opportunity for Reverend Lars."

"Perfect," Maria agreed. "Johann, find Albert and discuss our ideas. He should always be involved."

"On my way, Ma'ams."

Johann found Albert sitting in the garden. Heavy thoughts about the letter weighed on his mind. Hearing the new ideas temporarily distracted him.

"Johann, this is all good. We need to talk to Lars and have his input, too." Then, Albert clinched his jaw.

"Albert, is this one of those moments which requires the wisdom of the Lord?"

Albert locked eyes with Johann and shared some of the contents of the letter. Watching Johann's response, Albert related other information about Falke's connection to the castle. Johann's fists turned white. Remembering cooler heads prevail, he loosened up. "Albert, I'm here for you. You can trust me and my family. What do we need to do to prepare ourselves?"

"Maria knows about the letter, but Tea does not. We don't want her to be alarmed. We'll tell her later. Stefan is already taking precautions by placing guards on both sides of the river where the ferry is located. This man, Falke, has been dishonorable for a long time, but he has never hurt anyone before. His actions are escalating. When he approached your father and Benjamin, he made it a point to identify Ari as the father of your brothers. He probably has a scout in Christana and knows about you, too. I think I saw him in the church the day your father was baptized. He's unstable and unpredictable.

Traveling to and from Herrgott maybe too risky for our family as it is for Maria's father, King Stefan."

"That's why Maria was so quiet when she returned to the library. Tea and I noticed. We made a distraction to change the mood with a teacher-title list. They liked the title 'Ma'am.'"

"Quick thinking," Albert noted. "Speaking of teachers, we need to select tutors for you."

"Albert, could the Court Counselors tutor me? Maybe this is not the time to have new people coming to the palace."

Tilting his head, Albert looked at Johann and marveled at his words. "This is wise thinking, Johann. Each counselor has an expertise in a particular subject. I call on them often for ideas and opinions. They'll be honored to share their knowledge." Albert paused. "What should you be calling your new teachers? I don't advise calling them Ma'am," Albert teased while he admired his godson. "Come on. Let's go see how our 'Ma'ams' are doing."

Chapter 13

The Results

Ink dripped from the quills and stained their fingers. The scribes worked overtime copying the required pages for the students. Knowing several children and adults who could not read, the scribes gladly worked long hours without any complaints even though their fingers ached. Gathering all their work, the Head Scribe delivered the papers, and the counselors made the announcement.

Citizens of Christana
A school for reading is being established.
An assessment will be held for all children
ages six to sixteen.
Parents should bring their children to the Town Square
Saturday, November 30, at nine of the clock.

Word of the new school spread quickly. Several parents wanted their children to attend. Older children wanted to attend, too.

The parents and their children arrived early that Saturday morning. Wide-eyed boys and girls progressed through each station taking the tests until they could no longer master the skills. The counselors retained their papers, and the children scurried back to their parents.

The Head Counselor greeted each family. "The results will be revealed tomorrow at the end of Sunday's service." Anticipation grew. At least, they only had to wait one day.

* * *

Expecting a full house, Reverend Lars placed extra chairs at the back of the church. They quickly filled up. Even the innkeeper attended. Since he had locked his doors, his guests at the inn had no place to go. They came to church, too.

The parishioners enthusiastically offered praise songs to God. After Reverend Lars finished playing the organ, he approached the altar. His normal angelic composure gave presence to a somber face. Everyone gave their full attention as he did something very unusual. He used a visual aide.

Lars held up a sheet of paper and read off a few names, "King Albert, Queen Maria, Princess Dorothea, Johann, Ari, Magnus, Ivar, Oskar, Eva, Benjamin, Meta, Sarah, Klaus, Hans, Rolf, Lars..." The named group scrunched their eyebrows, wondering what they had in common. "There are many more names on this list, and it would take me a long time to read them all. Who wants to know the title of this list?"

Hands went up in the air. "I know the people on this list quite well. I have listened to their words, and more importantly, I have seen their actions and behaviors. The list is called the *Lamb's Book of Life*. The people named herein have a relationship with the Lord. If you're not sure your name is on the Lord's list, please come to see me after the service, and we'll pray. It's as easy as ABC. A—admit you are a sinner, that you need the Savior, and repent. B—believe that Jesus is the Son of God, died for your sins, and through His resurrection is your Savior. C—confess Jesus as Lord and ask Him to come into your life."

Lars laid the sheet of paper at the foot of the cross that hung on the wall and recited a verse from the Gospel of Johann (John). "For God so loved the world, that He gave His only begotten Son that who so ever believes in Him shall not perish, but have eternal life."

"Now, let's bow our heads and thank the Lord for this precious gift that is free to us, but cost Jesus His life."

Some worshipers prayed quietly. Some wept.

Lars continued to stand in the front of the church and reflected on the shortest sermon he had ever given. After a few moments, he nodded for the Court Counselors to come forward. He addressed the congregation one more time, "The counselors, also, have another important list of names."

The Head Counselor spoke for the group. "We have reviewed the results of the reading tests and found many levels of ability. Starting on Friday, each child will have their first day in the palace to meet their teacher, visit their room of learning, and receive their first lesson. Lessons will be one hour a day, Monday through Friday. You child's time is being posted on the announcement boards. Families with multiple children will have the same time. All school materials will be provided."

A low murmur rumbled through the church. The counselor continued, "There are two teachers. Princess Tea will be with the children ages six through ten." Immediately, the children of this age group smiled. "The children ages eleven through sixteen will be with Queen Maria." Now, the children of this age group smiled. "The children who read the sentences fluently will be working with the counselors. They'll help the younger ones as well as learn other subjects such as mathematics and science."

The parents beamed, but one congregant frowned and stood up. "What about the older ones?"

"What age are you referring to?" the counselor asked.

The man looked down and sheepishly responded, "I'm twenty-eight."

No one laughed. Several adults in the crowd could not read. Silence permeated the church. The counselors huddled together and discussed the situation. King Albert watched. The Head Counselor approached King Albert and whispered in his ear. The king smiled and nodded.

"We see there's a need for this age. Who shares this man's interest?" the counselor asked. Several older teenagers and adults raised their hands.

"Since this is a new process, could you wait a few weeks while everyone acclimates to our new school? Then, we can begin additional classes for those who are older than sixteen." All of them enthusiastically nodded. "Good, you have four days to prepare your children for their first day of school."

The church emptied quickly. Everyone left, except one. He approached the minister and asked, "I'm not sure if my name is in the Lamb's book. Will you pray with me?"

"Of course, Gunther," Lars replied. "The invitation is opened to everyone."

Thinking about the man that marred his face, Gunther absentmindedly reached up and rubbed his scar. "I have deep hurts in my life, and I have a tremendous hate for someone.

Will God still accept me?"

"The answer is still the same, yes. But, He wants you to give those burdens to Him. You have to forgive this person to receive true forgiveness from God."

"You don't understand. This man is no good. How can I forgive him?"

"Is he a sinner?" Lars asked.

"Definitely!"

"Are you a sinner?"

Lowering his eyes, Gunther reluctantly replied, "Uh, yes."

Lars laid his hand on Gunther's shoulder. "Sin is sin in God's eyes, and every sin needs forgiveness."

Gunther looked up at Lars. "When you put it that way, I want to get rid of this hate, but he's still ruthless."

"When you forgive him, it does not mean the other person changes their ways. The forgiveness releases you from the hate and anger in your heart, and lets God work on the other person's heart. You give God that burden, and He gives you freedom from it."

"Reverend, I'm ready."

Gunther received the Lord that day. Peace that he had never felt before filled his inner being like smoke filling the entire space inside a bottle. Lars noticed a difference in Gunther's face. Although his facial features looked the same, including the scar on his cheek, the rigid muscles softened, and a warm glow replaced the stern gaze in his eyes.

Chapter 14

Earning Trust

Curious parents meandered around the square forming a long line waiting for their turn to view the announcement board. The town crier stood close by for those who needed assistance to find their child's name. Klaus stared at the crowd. "Benjamin's son will attend this new school someday."

"Just about the same time my sons will be coming home," replied Ari. "I hope the time goes fast." Looking ahead, Ari began to walk faster. "We better hurry to the inn or we won't have a place to sit."

After eating, Klaus left to visit his family, but Ari stayed a little longer. King Albert walked by with two of his men. The banner tied to Ari's saddle caught his eye.

"Hello, Ari," Albert said walking up to his table. The guards stood by the doorway.

"Good to see you, King Albert," Ari replied being thankful he remembered to address the king in the proper way.

"Ari, I have some horse decisions to make. Could you share your expertise?"

"Of course. I'd be honored."

"Could you come tomorrow afternoon?"

"Yes, I'll be there," Ari replied.

"Good, see you then," said Albert, and he left with his men.

The following day, Ari kept wondering what horse decisions the king needed to make. "Wouldn't those decisions be up to the horse caretakers?" Ari prayed, "Lord, I pray I give the king good advice for the betterment of the king and our kingdom. In Your name, I pray. Amen."

Ari quit work early and prepared for his trip to the palace. "I get to be with Johann. I wonder how his studies are going?" he muttered. "I'm glad it's him and not me having to go to school." One last look in the mirror revealed a stubborn lock of curly hair that refused to stay in place. Ari sighed.

Inside the palace gate, one guard stepped forward and took Ari's horse while another escorted him to the garden where Albert sat.

Approaching footsteps caused Albert to lift his head. "Good day, Ari."

"Good day, King Albert." The guard nodded to the king and returned to his post.

Ari's eyes drifted from wall to wall taking in the enormity of the courtyard and palace.

Albert sensed Ari might be overwhelmed by the majesty of the palace and offered his prospective. "Ari, I often thank God for what I have. I was born into this family. It's a tremendous responsibility. I must take care of my family as well as every family in the entire kingdom."

"Albert, you're well thought of. I have heard travelers complaining about their rulers, but our people hold you in high esteem."

"The king is there for the people. The people are not there for the king. Respect is always earned. If it is lost, it takes much work to get it back. Sometimes, respect is lost forever." Albert regarded Ari's solemn face. "Speaking of respect, I would like for you to use your technique for gaining a horse's respect on some of my stock."

"I'd be honored, Albert. May I see the horses?"

"That would be a problem." Albert gave an impish grin.

"It's difficult to train a horse I cannot see."

"Ari, you'll see them but in due time. Please accompany me. I have something to show you."

Albert summoned Gunther to bring the Edelrosses. A smile

spread across Gunther's face, and he called for two other handlers to assist him.

A mesmerizing atmosphere surrounded the three horses, and Ari found his hand eager to rub their sleek necks. Albert watched his eyes. "As I mentioned before, these horses are the same breed. The white one is fully matured. The other two will eventually turn white as they get older. Gunther has grown up around these horses and loves them dearly."

Gunther turned his reddening face slightly away.

"Ari," Albert continued, "These three and the other horses in the stable are all stallions. When you came back from Herrgott, you brought back two mares. They, too, are Edelrosses."

Ari listened intently hoping to have an opportunity to work with a new breed of horse.

Pointing to the other side of the pasture, Albert drew Ari's attention to the new building. "We used the boards from the glass hill to build a stable for the mares. The stallions get a little frisky around the mares, so we keep them separated."

"I understand," Ari mused. "Guys do like to show off in front of the ladies. I did with Johanna."

Ari mention his wife's name. He must be more at peace with her passing, Albert surmised.

"May I examine one of the stallions?" Ari asked.

"Of course," Albert replied. "Gunther, have the handlers return the other two horses back to the stable."

The white horse stood still as Ari walked closer. *He's well trained and doesn't mind having a stranger near him,* Ari noted. "May I walk him?" Ari asked.

"Absolutely," Albert replied. Gunther handed Ari the lead rope. "This horse has talents and training that are very unusual. Gunther knows how to handle this breed. Let's walk him back to the stable."

Inside the stable, Ari slowed his pace past the stalls and studied the other horses more closely. "These look like some of the horses I trained on my farm."

"Good eye and memory. Most of these horses started at your farm," Albert confessed.

"You like my horses? How did you get them?"

"Your horses are the best. We found owners who were willing to trade. Now, let's go visit the ladies, the mare ladies."

Handing the reins to the caretaker, Gunther gave Ari a cold stare and returned the Edelross to his stall.

"Gunther, follow us to the other stable," Albert said. The caretaker walked behind Albert and Ari. Albert sensed the tension which tempted to fuel his suspicions toward Gunther.

Walking across the grassy pasture, Albert shared his vision. "I want to raise this breed of horse. Stefan and I share them. These Edelrosses will never be for sale. Gunther will need help with this process. In return, he'll teach you everything he knows about training them. Look at the two mares. Which one would you choose first?"

Ari examined both mares. "I'd start with the light gray one."

"That's Gunther's suggestion, too. Would you like to spend some time with Gunther before the evening meal?" Albert asked. "You two have so much in common."

"Yes. You can have Johann come and get me when it's time."

Albert nodded and returned to the palace. Gunther cocked an eyebrow and looked suspiciously at Ari. *You're not a royal. How will you behave now that there's no one watching?*

"Gunther, I was thanking the Lord earlier today that I wouldn't be going to school like Johann. God must have been laughing when He heard my prayer. He knew I would want to learn from you." Ari straightened up and bowed. "Your student is ready."

Gunther's head pulled back a bit, his eyes widening. *Did Ari just humble himself? Perhaps, I can trust this man.*

"I have so many questions, Gunther. Please be patient with me."

Tiny wrinkles formed around Gunther's eyes, pulling the

corners of his mouth upward. "I had to watch for several years before I was allowed to handle these horses by myself. You'll learn faster than I did. Let's go fetch the white stallion."

Ari chuckled. Gunther put unusual equipment on the Edelross and guided him into the corral. This time Ari sat on the rails. Gunther walked next to the horse using extra, long reins for a few laps. He lifted his hands in the air and gave an order while holding the long reins. The mighty stallion reared up on his hind legs. When he came down, he walked a few steps backward.

When Ari clapped his hands, the horse started to rear up on his hind legs. Gunther quickly pulled on the long reins to control the stallion.

"I'm sorry," Ari apologized.

"It wasn't you, Ari. He can get startled sometimes. Let's go curry him and let him rest."

"May I curry him for you?"

"Of course," Gunther replied with another stunned look. "He wants to do this lowly work?" he whispered.

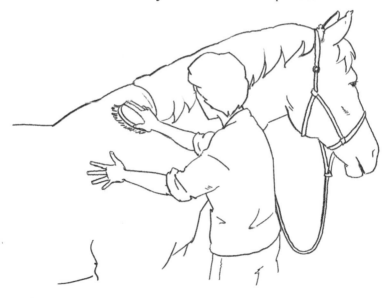

Ari's hand slid across the back of the horse following the

contour of the firm muscles. He wanted the horse to get accustomed to his touch. Gunther watched how Ari took his time, making eye contact and rubbing each side of the horse with the back of the brush before the currying started. *Ari can teach me some things, too,* Gunther admitted to himself.

"Gunther, do you miss your home in Herrgott?" Ari asked.

"I used to miss it years ago, but I like it here. I feel safe."

Ari gave him a puzzled look. *Why did he say that?*

Ari started to say something, but Gunther continued talking. "When King Albert and Queen Maria came here years ago, I was one of the attendants. I was young and had never been away from home before. After a few years, I missed my family, and I returned to Herrgott. There's a man there I don't like. I used to hate him."

"If I may ask, what happened?"

"I gave the hate to God, and He kept it. I don't want that feeling anymore, but I don't trust that man. He's still no good."

"I had the same problem, Gunther. I had to seek God for help in my life. I wish I had repented sooner, but His ways are higher than our ways. We have to have faith and trust in Him."

Gunther rubbed the scar on his face, contemplating Ari's words. "This is my constant reminder of this ruthless man. He wanted me to work for him, and he didn't like my answer. I feel safe here."

Ari didn't know why, but he followed the urge in his gut. He walked over to Gunther like a father, put his arms around Gunther's neck, and hugged him. Gunther offered no resistance. He had just shared his inner secret and needed positive affirmation. The two horsemen became true friends that day.

Gunther's nose twitched, and he stepped aside. "Ari, if you are going to eat with the royal family, you better clean up. You smell like a horse." Ari looked at Gunther and chuckled. Gunther joined him.

"Papa?" Johann's voice came from the front of the stable. "It's time for the evening meal. Are you ready?"

"Almost, Son, I need to clean up first." He turned around and looked warmly at Gunther and winked at him. Gunther shook his head and rolled his eyes.

Chapter 15

New Arrival

The younger children hid behind their mothers' skirts, but the older ones wanted to go alone. On the first day of school, the students walked in quiet awe to the front gate where the counselors waited to verify their names and schedule times. Once inside, the children's eyes widened to capture the new surroundings.

Princess Tea smoothed her dress one more time before her students arrived. Each boy bowed and each girl curtseyed as they passed their teacher. Smiles filled their faces as they entered their classroom. Tables and chairs made to accommodate their small bodies waited for them.

The children sat down quietly, their eyes following their new teacher as she walked to the front of the room. "Boys and girls, welcome to your first day of school. In this classroom, I will be your teacher, and you will be my students. My proper title as your teacher is Ma'am. When we're not in school, my proper title is Princess Dorothea."

"Today," Tea continued, "we'll get acquainted with each other, our room, and do a lesson. Any questions?"

The children remained quiet. *Maybe, the parents have told their children not to talk,* she surmised and thought of a quick solution to get the children to open up. "I have two chickens and one duck. How many horses can I get in a trade?" she asked.

"Are the horses alive?" one boy questioned.

"Why do you ask?" Tea responded with an inquisitive look.

"Well, Ma'am," the boy replied, "no one will trade a live

horse for only three birds." The boys laughed, and the girls giggled.

"Good observation," Tea noted while passing out quills. "I want to take you with me when I go horse trading." The children giggled again.

"Now, look at this feather. Who can tell me what animal it came from?

Several children blurted out duck. "Hmm, do you think that response was a little noisy?"

"Yes," several children responded.

"Let's make it a rule that only one person can answer at a time. Raise your hand so I know you want to offer an answer, and I'll choose one person at a time to talk."

Tea held the quill up again. Her fingers demonstrated how the tip had been cut at an angle. Then, she dipped the quill in a jar of dark liquid. Carefully, Tea wrote one of the children's name on the paper. "Who is Hans?"

Hans raised his hand. "This is your name, Hans. Would you like to write your name, too?"

Hans face lit up like a candle. "Yes!"

The other children looked at Tea with longing eyes. "Children, if you would like to write your name, quietly raise your hand." All hands went up. Tea smiled. *Mission accomplished.* "Splendid," Tea said. "When you receive your paper, trace your letters with your pointing finger like this."

Index fingers rose on several hands. The youngest students copied their older peers. Class assistants read the students' names and passed out their papers. Helpers distributed bottles of ink for the children to dip their quills into and try to mimic the straight and curved lines of the letters. Smiles appeared all over the room.

Each child examined their work as they finished their name. Smiles of approval spread across their faces. Afterward, Tea guided the children to a corner of the room. One by one, the students introduced themselves.

Tea delighted in each student as they talked. *Children are a blessing,* she thought with a sigh.

At the end of the introductions, Tea noticed two boys playing foot tag and three girls yawning. "Let's return to our chairs."

One boy sat down and blurted, "The ink has dried."

"You don't have to have quills and ink to write your name," Tea informed. "Does anyone have a suggestion what else we could use?"

"I use a stick to draw in the dirt. I could use the stick to make letters," one student proudly announced.

"Excellent idea, Hans. Any other suggestions?" Hans's face beamed when Tea praised his answer.

"Sometimes I play in the ashes with my finger. I could make letters in the ashes," another student offered.

Tea's eyes sparkled. "Sarah, this is another excellent idea. If you didn't want to put your finger in the ashes, what else could you use?"

"Hans' stick, if he'll let me borrow it."

Laughter flooded the room. Tea looked up to the ceiling and quietly chuckled. "Hans, do you have an extra stick for Sarah that she could borrow?" Hans nodded. "Wonderful, Sarah, if you cannot find another stick, Hans has one for you. You all have work to do this weekend. Practice writing your name. We'll meet again the day after Sunday. You're dismissed."

Each student stood up and proudly picked up their paper. "Thank you, Ma'am. See you Monday," they said, exiting the room. Once outside, the children ran as fast as they could to their mothers and bragged about writing their names. Tea watched them from the window. Her smile surpassed the children's.

Maria walked in. "How did the first day of class go?"

"Mama, I have only one regret. I wish we would have started a school sooner. How was your class?"

"My class was wonderful. The children enjoyed writing with the ink and quills. Daughter, we need to rest up. The next group will be here shortly."

Tea continued to look outside. "I could do this all day."

* * *

The scribes were constantly copying materials for the teachers. At times, their fingers ached, but they never complained until the day the printing press arrived.

Albert noticed that the once jovial group of scribes had become sullen and moody. "I wonder what the problem is?" he muttered grasping his chin. "I need a helpful strategy."

The aroma of sweet treats floated from the basket Albert carried into the workroom. The scribes' eyes brightened, and their mouths watered. "Men, the cooks made these fresh for you today. They appreciate what you're doing. Some of the students are their children."

"Your Majesty," began one of the scribes. Immediately, worried looks covered the other scribes' faces. They shook their heads, and the speaker fell silent.

"Yes," King Albert said, "go on."

The brave scribe lowered his head and responded, "We love

what we're doing, and we're going to miss it dearly when the printing press takes over our jobs." He gave a deep sigh and kept his head lowered.

"Is that it? Is that why you've been gloomy?"

"Yes," they all replied.

"Thank you. I thought it was something serious," Albert said.

"Losing this task is serious," another brave scribe added.

"You are scribes. There will always be a demand for your skills. But the demand for copies of the curriculum will be greater than what you'll be able to print. We need the printing press."

"But your Majesty, we enjoy being part of the learning process," another scribe pleaded.

"The printing press won't work by itself, and I didn't hire outside printers. Do you know of anyone who would like to run the press? It takes knowledgeable people who know how to spell words and make spaces between those words."

The scribes' eyes all widened at the same time and fixated on the king. Albert hummed a familiar happy tune, reached in the basket for a tasty treat, and carried the basket around to each scribe. One by one, the scribes reached in and took a pastry without taking their eyes off the king. King Albert winked at them and left the basket on the table.

Halfway down the hallway, he raised his arms up high. "I wish all the problems were as easy as this one to fix, Thank you, Lord."

Chapter 16

New Opportunity

The flame flickered when Ivar turned the page of his book. Staring at the candle, he rubbed his eye. The other hand reached up to muffle a yawn. "Magnus, what's the word for sleep?"

"I didn't memorize that one," Magnus replied. "We don't have time for it anyway."

Magnus memorized long lists of words, but he had trouble using the correct grammar. Ivar could use proper grammar but not the correct words. Both brothers used their strengths to help each other.

A year had gone by since Magnus and Ivar had first come to the University. They had become fluent enough in the new language to take all their courses with the rest of the student ministers. The University of Herrgott granted them formal admission.

"Ivar, we're in! Let's celebrate and go for a walk," Magnus suggested.

"Good idea."

Strolling down the sidewalk, they noticed two men standing in the street and speaking in low voices. When Magnus and Ivar passed them, the men stopped talking. The brothers recognized one as a local citizen, but the other man looked unfamiliar. At least, Magnus and Ivar had never seen him before in Herrgott or in the church. Magnus dismissed the whole incident, but something rose up uncomfortably inside of Ivar. So, he prayed, "Lord, if there is something You want me to know, teach me."

* * *

A month had passed and the new duty roster was posted. Magnus elbowed Ivar and they both grinned from ear to ear as they discovered their new assignment. Gardening meant they would be working outside instead of doing the more tedious indoor chores.

Ivar entered the storage shed first. The musty smell offended his nose. Picking up the shovel he shook his head. "What happened to this?" He offered the broken tool to his brother, but Magnus backed away. Reluctantly, Ivar walked to the carpenter's shop with the broken shovel. In the distance, he spotted the stranger. Ivar recognized him with his dark hair and cold eyes. He tried to blend in with the crowd but failed. The stranger approached him.

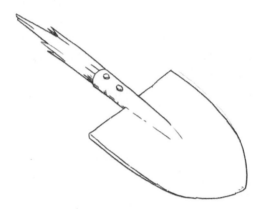

"I see you're a laborer," the stranger said. "You probably don't get paid enough for your hard work."

Ivar chose his words carefully. "I don't get paid, but I do get a place to stay and food to eat."

"I want to offer you an opportunity to earn good money. You'll have a place to stay and all the food you want to eat." The stranger examined Ivar from head to toe. "And better clothes then those rags."

"Your offer is tempting. If I'm interested, how will I get in contact with you?"

"I'll be here the first Monday of each month for a while. The opportunity is opened to any of your friends that are not treated fairly such as yourself."

Ivar nodded his understanding and continued to the carpenter's shop without committing to anything. The stranger lost interest and began scouting the crowd for another prospect to approach.

Cold chills ran down Ivar's spine, and he prayed, "Lord, this does not sound promising. What should I do? Open a door for me."

A royal guard entered the carpenter's shop with a similar problem as Ivar's—a broken tool. Ivar approached the guard. "If someone wanted to be a sentry, how do you apply for the job?"

"Do you have time right now?" the guard asked.

"Yes, I do."

The guard handed his axe to the carpenter and then motioned to Ivar. "Good, follow me."

Oh no, Ivar thought. *The stranger is he still out there! Can't be seen with this guard.*

Squinting his eyes, the guard studied Ivar's face wondering why the pause.

"May I talk to the carpenter first and then meet you at the palace gate?"

"Yes," the guard replied relaxing his eyes. "I'll be waiting for you."

Ivar heaved a huge sigh and finished his task with the carpenter. He noticed the stranger walking in the opposite direction. Ivar hurried to the palace and quickly located the friendly guard, who promptly escorted him into the palace grounds. As he walked near the garden area, King Stefan noticed Ivar and his unusual clothing.

"Are you one of the ministry students?" King Stefan asked.

Ivar's eyes widened. He momentarily fumbled his words and gave an awkward bow. "Yes, Your Highness."

"I have a question about the Bible to ask. Do you have time?"

The guard bowed to the king and left the two alone. "Does God always hear our prayers and answer them?" King Stefan asked with a troubled look.

Whoa, thought Ivar, *this is a tough one. Lord, I need Your wisdom.* He took a deep breath and responded, "May we both sit down, Sire?"

"Certainly. In the matters of God, we are both equals."

Amazing reply, Lord, Ivar marveled. *Now, help me with the king's question.* "Sire, you're a father. As a father, did your child ask you for things."

"Of course, children are always asking for something. You'll find that out someday."

"Did you always give your child everything that was requested?" Ivar probed further.

"No, I did not." Stefan sighed. "Some requests were inappropriate for that age. Some requests were never beneficial at any age, and the request was denied."

"Was your decision always respected?"

"Unfortunately, no. Sometimes, my decisions have caused me personal heartbreak. Sometimes, being a parent is harder than being a king. I have to judge what is best and what is not."

"Sire, you have answered your own question."

Stefan marveled at his words and proposed, "When you're finished with your studies, could you stay in Herrgott as one of our ministers?"

"I'm honored by your offer, Sire, but I want to return to my hometown. My brother has offered me a position there. He's waiting for me to return and perform his marriage ceremony."

"Your brother is a blessed man. What's his name?"

Now, Ivar started to turn red in the face. Stefan noticed and looked sternly at him increasing those furrows between his eyebrows. "Johann," Ivar said softly.

"And the bride's name?" Stefan pressed leaning forward.

"Tea," Ivar responded and looked away at the same time.

"You're Ari's son?"

The mood changed. "Yes, I am," Ivar replied with wide eyes.

Stefan stood up. Ivar stood up. "Welcome to the family. Tea is my granddaughter!"

Ivar took a deep breath and slowly released it. "Thank you, Sire."

"You're family. Call me Stefan. Proper protocol requires using the titles of respect when in the company of nonfamily or in referring to the title holder to others."

"Sire," Ivar started, "Stefan, if I heard something disturbing and suspicious, would you want to know?"

The mood changed again, and Stefan sat down. "Yes, I want to know."

Ivar shared about his encounter with the stranger and what he had witnessed the previous month. Stefan leaned back in his chair and pondered on the information. Finally, he asked, "Who else have you shared this with?"

"You're the only one. I was careful with the guard and pretended I was looking for information about employment as a sentry. I was hoping to find someone in authority after I was in the palace walls."

"Smart man," Stefan noted. "Ari told me you have a twin brother. This stranger may approach him thinking it is you. Your brother needs to be aware of what you shared. Other than him, tell no one. Do not share with anyone at the University or include it in any letters you may write."

"Stefan, I prayed for the Lord to help me immediately after the encounter with the stranger. Your guard walked into the same shop where I was. After I talked to him, he invited me to come to the palace. That's how I got here."

"That explains it. Earlier, I had an unusual desire to go for a walk outside. The Lord provides."

"Johann says that many times."

"My Tea has chosen wisely. Their marriage will be a blessing to everyone."

"Stefan, you can trust my family. I felt this man was not honorable and was trying to recruit workers under a cover of secrecy. What troubles me more is what the job requires. He did not say, and I didn't ask."

Stefan leaned forward. The furrows between his eyebrows dug in deeper. "What did he look like?"

"Clean shaven, short dark hair, about my height and build. He wore decent but common clothes."

Stefan leaned back studied Ivar's face. He wasn't comfortable revealing his true suspicions, so he offered something that might explain Ivar's unease. "There's always a possibility of overthrowing a kingdom. Since this man is only coming once a month, he may be gradually building up a power base. His recruits may not know what the true motives are until it's too late. We need to keep our trust in God for His protection and will."

Ivar thanked Stefan for his time. When he started to leave, the guard approached him. "If you're interested in being a sentry, there are positions open. Trustworthy men are given top priority. Unfortunately, you would not have time for any other occupation."

"This is an important decision. I need time to contemplate what direction I need to follow," Ivar replied.

"I understand," the guard acknowledged and escorted Ivar to the palace gate.

Walking to the carpenter's shop, Ivar saw the stranger approaching another man. *I pray he didn't see me leaving the palace,* he thought. *I sense this man is connected to trouble.*

Ivar retrieved his repaired shovel and returned to his garden. Shutting the gate, he looked up. The stranger had followed him but kept walking. The hair on Ivar's arms rose.

Ivar obeyed the king's request. He shared with Magnus about the conversation with the stranger, the king, and the palace guard.

"Ivar, this is serious. I'll be careful if I see this man again. Does he know your name?"

"He didn't ask. The king's concern is that he may see you as me not knowing we're twins."

"We have to be careful near the first of each month and avoid walking together. If he's dishonorable, he may be suspicious of anyone that doesn't accept his invitation. Are you now considering staying in Herrgott?" Magnus asked.

"My first goal is to finish my education and training," Ivar replied. "Where that leads me will be determined later."

Chapter 17

The Stranger

Evening shadows draped over the buildings as the shopkeepers closed their doors for the night. The stranger scanned the street one more time and headed to an unpaved path. Four men, huddling near a thicket of bushes and trees, waited for him. Under the cloak of darkness, they traveled farther down the path. They camped in the refuge of the forest and settled down for the night. One of the men took the first watch while the others went to sleep.

A noise woke the stranger. He noticed everyone was asleep including the man on watch who was leaning against a tree. Quietly, he stood up and approached the watchman. Finding a small branch lying on the ground, he picked it up and with a casualness that told of much practice, he struck the man across the face, sending the hapless man sprawling into the underbrush with a cry of pain. Blood trickled down his face.

"Get up, before I let you have it again," the stranger ordered.

"Ow," The injured man hollered rubbing his aching head. His eyes bulged and he scrambled to his feet.

With his arm cocked, the stranger got right in the recruit's face. "When you work for me, you follow orders!"

"Yes, sir," the man groveled.

The commotion had woken the other men. Two of them laughed. The other man remained quiet. The stranger pointed to the quiet one. "Stay awake. You're next."

The two laughing men, the injured man, and the stranger went back to sleep. The quiet man stayed awake, wondering what he had gotten himself involved in.

A few hours later, the quiet man tapped the shoulder of one of the men who had laughed. "It's your turn." The just woken man scowled at the recruit and rolled over. Unfortunately, the stranger woke up and saw it. Kicking the uncooperative man in the arm, he warned him, "Be disobedient again, and your pay will be less. The recruit glared but remained silent as he left to stand watch. His ego was more bruised than his aching arm.

The night passed without further incident, and daylight broke the darkness, waking everyone up. The other laughing man made a fire and prepared the food. He smacked his neck in a futile effort to ward off the irritating insects that buzzed around his face.

At length, they set out amid the swarms of insects and trekked through the forest. The recruits had never been this far from their city. The stranger walked behind them, watching their every move.

"Where are we going?" the young man with the bloodied head asked.

"You'll find out soon enough," the stranger announced. "Now, be quiet, or I'll let my stick do the talking for me again."

Searching for signs of the path in the thick vegetation, the men frowned at each other but held their tongues. Tree limbs hung down and occasionally smacked someone in the face. Bushes grew close to the dirt path and sometimes grew over the trail making it difficult to walk. The stranger knew where to go and pointed out the correct direction when necessary.

The sound of moving water drifted through the woods, increasing with each step. After trudging around a tall thicket of bushes, they saw a river. All gave a sigh of relief.

"We're back to the Herrgott River," the stranger said. Farther on, a large tributary joined with the Herrgott River. "This other river is called Vogel. Both rivers are important. You'll learn why after we cross to the other side. Men, look over there."

The recruits spotted something emerging from the tree line on the opposite side of the river. Ramparts outlined the tops of stone walls. Towers jutted out on the corners. At the edge of the riverbank nearest them, a moored rowboat rocked back and forth. The smell of river water replaced the odor of the earthy forest.

Embarking the boat, the stranger took his position in the bow while the recruits sat down and picked up the oars. "Men, it's time to earn your wages. Let's go to the other side where you'll have a better life."

Growls erupted and they snarled at each other. The land-lovers bumped oars in an uncoordinated attempt to row. They adjusted their motions and rowed together in proper rhythm. A smirky smile grew on their faces. Squinting one eye, the stranger mused, *Working as a team, good sign.*

Two guards waited on the other side. Fighting the river's current, the oarsmen strained to row the boat close to the dock. The stranger threw a rope, and the attending guards secured the boat.

One of the guards opened his mouth to say something, but the stranger looked him in the eye and shook his head. The guard quietly backed up. The recruits eyed the clean and well-groomed, uniformed guards. Then they looked at their own clothes, dirty and tattered.

The stranger addressed his recruits one more time, "Welcome to Falke Castle. These gentlemen will show you where you can clean up and put on your new clothes. Afterward, you'll meet the other gentlemen who live and work here."

Carefully laid stones provided a direct path to the castle. The ominous fortress stood alone. A banner, mounted over the gate, fluttered in the wind, occasionally revealing the insignia of a hawk.

Acknowledging the signal from the stranger, the ironclad portcullis slowly ascended, and the wooden doors behind it swung open. The guards on duty scrutinized the new recruits walking into the castle. Once inside, the clacking sound of the heavy grate descending mesmerized the new recruits causing them to flinch when the pointed ends of the portcullis struck the ground. The attending guards closed and bolted the wooden doors sharing a quiet snicker.

The stranger went one way and the recruits followed the guards in a different direction. The accommodations intrigued the new recruits noting that they would have a roof over their heads that would not leak and clean beds to sleep in.

"Are you hungry?" one of the guards asked.

"Yes," the four recruits answered simultaneously.

"After you clean up and change clothes, we'll take you to the dining hall."

The recruits admired their new clothes as they quietly followed the guards down the hallway. The group walked into an enormous room. Matching fireplaces flanked each end of the dining hall. A warm glow illuminated the area and provided warmth. Many other guards sat around the table waiting for the new recruits. After everyone was seated, a finely dressed man entered the room. A servant, carrying a hawk on a gloved hand, followed.

"Good evening, everyone," he addressed the group of uniformed guards. "A special welcome to our new recruits."

The new recruits sat at the far end of the table, but they could see the finely dressed man very clearly. The stranger, they had been traveling with through the woods, had changed his clothes.

"Gentlemen, enjoy your dinner."

"Thank you, Falke," the men replied.

The recruits felt a little embarrassed. The stranger, who offered them good wages, who offered them a better life, who lead them through the woods, and who had to discipline them during the night, was the owner of this castle and their master. Their attitude changed that night. They lifted their mugs and pledged their loyalty to Falke.

Falke smiled and nodded in approval. *They never see this*

coming. How easy it is to manipulate the minds of the unsuspecting and the uneducated.

The hawk stood still on the perch as the servant tethered the leather straps on its legs to the pole. Falke rubbed his hawk's head and offered the bird raw meat to eat.

Chapter 18

The Lessons of Life

Tap, *tap, tap. Tap, tap, tap.* Staring at his plate of food, Johann unconsciously drummed his fingers on the table. *What's that word? Kirche!* He proceeded to use it in a sentence using the Herrgott language. Tea covered her mouth and giggled. Johann cocked his eyebrow and threw her an odd look.

"I'm sorry, Johann, but it sounded funny," Tea apologized.

"What was so funny?"

"You just said, 'Let's plant a church tree in the garden.' I think a cherry tree would be more beneficial."

Ari looked up. A vision of Magnus and Ivar learning Herrgott popped into his mind. *What if one of the twins decided to live there? I'd need to know how to talk with his family.* He set his fork down and asked, "Could I learn this language, too?"

"Ari, Maria and I will help you," Albert offered. "You also have a teacher with you when you're working with the horses."

"Gunther," replied Ari. "He's from Herrgott and a good teacher. Thank you, Albert. Johann, let's take a walk in the garden and find a good place for the church tree."

Johann's face turned a little red again. Ari grinned and wrapped his arm around his son's shoulder. "Let's go."

"Wait," said Albert. "I'll join you."

With his back toward Albert, Ari's lip twitched in frustration.

Walking to the garden, Ari watched the furrows on Albert's face increase. *This is more than a causal walk. I hope I can help.*

115

Albert chose a secluded place and motioned for everyone to be seated. Thick tension filled the air, warning Ari and Johann to wait for Albert to talk.

"My soul is very distraught. I need to hear other opinions, but I have to be careful with the discussions. What I'll share with you cannot be repeated to anyone." Albert's chest swelled with a deep breath. "I have received a letter informing me of the actions of a person near Herrgott. He may be amassing an army. We can't be sure since his men are sequestered in his castle. He's very controlling and effective in developing loyalty. Ari, a stranger tried to recruit Ivar. It is possible this unknown person is connected to this castle."

Ari's eyes narrowed as he stood up. "What did he do to my son? I'll go right now."

"Ivar is safe. He confided with Stefan about a man promising many benefits if he would follow him. Your son behaved wisely and found a way, with the help of the Lord, to speak to Stefan privately. If you write letters to your sons, never include anything about the activities of this palace, the families here, or your connection to it. Never mention Johann in your letters for his safety and yours."

As Ari sat down, he hung his head to think. "Could the man with the hawk have anything to do with this?"

"Yes," Albert continued. "The man called Falke is the owner of the castle on the Herrgott River. Did you see it on your journey?"

"Benjamin and I passed it in the dark going to Herrgott. On our return trip, the captain of the guard pointed to the converging river and the castle."

"This castle serves the owner where these two rivers meet. All vessels must pay a toll to use these rivers. This is how he makes his income. Unfortunately, he overcharges. Boat captains have no recourse. They have to pay to continue, or their goods will be confiscated."

"Why does he want an army?" Ari asked. "Why is he interested in my family?"

"Good questions, Ari. I don't know his true intentions, but they're not honorable. I have my suspicions he has an informant here in Christana. That's why we have to be careful when we discuss this matter. Someone with ill intentions could be listening."

"Albert, you're asking for opinions. I want to offer mine."

"Please continue."

"If there's a possibility of an army coming here, we should be prepared. Do we have the proper equipment? Are the guards trained for battle? Are the horses trained for battle?"

"Ari, this confirms my thoughts. I was contemplating the same questions. It will take a few years for Falke to amass and train soldiers. We have plenty of time to prepare."

"Magnus and Ivar will be finished with their education and training by that time," Johann added.

"There's the possibility he may just want to be a bully and pick on people," Albert surmised. "We suspect it was he who scratched up the ferryman's face and hands with his hawk last year."

"I saw him after he was attacked. Is that why the guards escorted us to the ferry?" Ari asked.

"Yes, and the guards are still there," Albert added. "The ferry and its owner are important to Stefan."

Movement behind a bush caught Ari's attention. "Albert, Johann, I need to attend the horses. I'll be back shortly."

Peeking his head around the manicured bushes, Ari spotted Gunther walking to the horse gate. Ari waited until Gunther had entered the gate before he proceeded any further. Once inside the gate, he found Gunther sitting on a bench with his head hanging down.

He looked up and saw Ari standing next to him. "You didn't say anything about what happened to me. You didn't repeat my deep hurt."

"Gunther, I'm your friend. I would never betray your confidence. How could you be connected to any of this?"

"Ari," Gunther said pointing to his scar, "Falke is the one who did this to me. Gustav, the owner of the ferry, is my uncle. He raised me when my parents died in a wagon accident. Falke attacked my uncle, my family! King Albert needs to know what happened. Would you tell him for me?"

"Yes, but, it would be better if he heard it from you."

"Will you go with me?"

"Yes, my friend. I am here for you. Let's go."

Not long after, Gunther stood in front of Albert. He stared at the ground, trying to build up his nerve. He slowly lifted his eyes and told the king about the man who cut his face. When he finished talking, he took a deep breath and said, "I'm so sorry."

Albert walked over to Gunther and whispered something in

his ear as he embraced him. Taking a step backward he said, "Gunther, you'll always be safe here at Christana. Your uncle is safe, too. There are guards on both sides of the river. They have built permanent stone buildings to live in. You and your uncle are important to us."

A small measure of peace entered Gunther. "Thank you, Sire."

Albert pondered on the information. *Hawk man, will you become more aggressive? I pray you don't.*

The sound of bubbling water of a nearby fountain brought back a childhood memory to Johann. His grandmother sat on the bench next to him saying her memorable words. He unconsciously uttered them out loud, "The Lord provides."

Albert looked at Johann accepting this word of truth. "Yes, yes He does. Thank You, Lord. I needed that." Feeling refreshed, Albert stood up and left.

Chapter 19

Recruitments

He sat in his chair reminiscing about the people that raised him. Stroking his new beard, Falke resolved that life made him into the man he was. He gloated about his leadership skills and watched his army grow. "Patience is a virtue," he muttered. "I can wait for the right time."

He had craftily approached his targets. With sympathy and promises of a better life, Falke had ensnared discontented young men to join him. Arriving at the castle, the new recruits were full of wonder and excitement at the opportunity to visit such a mysterious place. None of them had ever seen the confluence of the two rivers.

Falke complimented the attending guards as he walked along the rampart. A boat stopping to pay the toll caught his eye. He cocked his eyebrow and hurried down the stairs to greet the unsuspecting crew.

* * *

Albert peeked into the library. *No one's here,* he thought. He nestled into the chair by the window and opened his book. Sunrays illuminated the pages. He scrunched his face at the sound of footsteps that edged closer to his chair.

"Your Majesty," the guard began, "there's a visitor, a young man, that requests an audience with you."

"What is the nature of his calling?" Albert asked, adjusting his facial expression.

"The man was extorted, Your Majesty."

Immediately, a queasy feeling attacked Albert's gut. "I will meet with him in the throne room. Wait until I call for him before you bring the visitor in. Have Johann and the counselors meet me there."

The guard bowed. The two men headed in opposite directions. Albert's footsteps echoed as he walked into the empty throne room. He stopped and prayed, "Father, I do not know what will be revealed today. I ask for your guidance and discernment of this man's knowledge and intentions. Help me to follow the right decisions that will protect the people You have put in my care. This I ask in Your name. Amen."

The counselors entered with Johann and stood to the side. Albert motioned for Johann to sit in the chair next to his own. Taking charge of this meeting, King Albert gave the guard a nod to bring in the visitor.

The visitor's downcast eyes and pale face portrayed a troubled young man. He approached the throne in a proper and respectful manner. First, he bowed to King Albert, then to Johann, and finally to the counselors. After he had finished the customary acknowledgements, the visitor began his oration. "Your Majesty, allow me to introduce myself. I am Alexander from the village of Himmel. It's on the Vogel River several days ride from the Herrgott River."

"I have heard of this village. What brings you to Christana?"

"I was with my uncle's boat on the Vogel River. When we reached the Herrgott River, we stopped to pay the customary toll. A finely dressed man met us at the river's edge and came on board. He pointed to a few of our young men and invited us to his castle. My uncle has traveled this river many times and had never seen this man before. He was curious and nodded for us to follow him."

Then Alexander's tone of voice changed and became halted. He paused several times trying to explain what happened next. All eyes intently watched him and everyone strained their ears to detect his accented words. "The finely dressed man made comments about how we were not being treated fairly by our captain. He asked if any of us wanted to work for him. One of the young men raised his hand and said he would and shared that the captain was my uncle."

At this point, Alexander trembled. He took a deep breath and continued, "The finely dressed man took me to the side and threatened to sink my uncle's boat if we did not deliver a recruit to him each time we pass his castle heading north. After I told my uncle what the man had threatened, he wished that he had never allowed us to disembark his boat."

Alexander's face lightened up, and he smiled. "About one day later, we came to the ferry. The ferryman noticed my worried face and asked if he could help. I don't know why, but I told him everything. He suggested I talk to the king of Christana and a man named Ari. He said they might be able to help." Alexander looked directly into Albert's eyes and pleaded, "Can you help us? Do you know this man, Ari? Can he help us?"

King Albert took a deep breath. "How long ago did this meeting at the castle take place?"

"Seven days ago. After we reached our destination, my uncle stayed in port to load the goods to transport back down the river. He allowed me some time off while we are in port. I came here as fast as I could."

"Who knows why you came to Christana?"

"Only my uncle knows. He's the only one I told about the threat on his boat and the ferryman's advice."

"You have done well to come. You're safe here. My guards will escort you back to your uncle tomorrow. You may stay here as my guest."

"Thank you, Your Majesty. You are most kind."

After the young man departed, Albert asked his counselors to come closer. "This news troubles my soul. It's time for you to know everything I know about this situation. I need advice from you, and I need wisdom from God."

The counselors listened to King Albert. They soon realized everyone's safety could be in jeopardy if this man amassed an army and attacked the palace. They offered several suggestions. After pondering on them, Albert realized it was time to increase his military.

"A tormentor never starts a fight without the confidence he can win," Albert said. "We must anticipate that his target is us. We must prepare ourselves."

"Our coffers have a surplus due to the growth of the kingdom," the Head Counselor said. "We can hire and train more guards. We could use more horses."

Johann leaned over and whispered to Albert, "My father has several horses that are currently being saddle broke." Albert looked at Johann and smiled.

"Gentlemen," King Albert began, "we have many talented men in Christana. We'll start our recruitment process immediately. I'll make plans to provide more horses."

Albert and Johann headed for the stable and found Ari working with the black stallion. The horse balked, rotated his ears back, and turned his head away. Ari jiggled the lead rope fastened to the halter. Temporally startled, the horse complied and followed the command of the new trainer.

"Papa," Johann began, grinning broadly, "what's easier, training you or training the horse?"

"Right now," Ari confided, "we're equal. My horses are easier to train, because these skills are unusual and it takes more practice." Ari gave the reins to Gunther who got the horse to raise up on his back legs. While still standing, the horse gave a kick.

Albert watched his prized horse with longing eyes wishing he could take a ride and leave his troubles behind but duty called.

"Ari," Albert said, "I have something to ask. Do you have time?"

"I have to ask my boss first," Ari replied with a wink to Gunther.

Gunther rolled his eyes and slowly shook his head as he

watched the three men walking away. Turning around, Gunther smiled all the way to the stable.

Albert pondered about telling Ari everything, but hesitated. "Ari, we're going to recruit more guards, and we need more horses. Do you know where I might find some saddle broke horses?"

Ari smiled. "How many do you need?"

"Ten for now, and more in the future."

"I can take care of that for you. I'll go see how those horses are doing right now." Ari departed and contemplated why the horses were needed. *Is this because of the hawk man?*

* * *

The counselors compiled a list of character traits that would determine the qualifications for new guards. After much debate, they narrowed down the list: loyal, trustworthy, and courageous. All applicants must be twenty years old or older and be a citizen of Christana.

The posting of the job position created quite a stir in the town square. Many young men wanted the opportunity for good pay and job security. Young looking applicants had to bring proof to verify their age. Baptismal papers sufficed. Lars kept busy going through the files looking for the records.

One by one, the counselors interviewed the applicants asking about their skills and observing their behavior. As usual, they used check-off lists.

This time, the scribes utilized the printing press to make multiple copies for the guard applications. In the beginning, the scribes made many mistakes as well as getting their fingers pinched. Through trial and error, they exceeded their own expectations and became quite proficient.

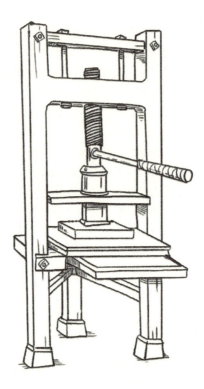

After hours of discussion, the counselors called for all the applicants and announced their selections. "There are thirty openings at this time," the Head Counselor informed. "The remaining applicants will be considered for the next round of enlistment for guard duty."

Frowns spread on the faces of those who had to wait. They murmured as they exited through the horse gate. One of them turned around and came back to the selected group. "Are we training to be guards or soldiers?"

"Good question," the Head Counselor said. "What does a guard do?"

"They watch over people or property and keep them safe," the young man replied.

"Good answer. What if the person the guard is watching over is in danger?"

"They defend that person. That's their sworn duty."

"Well said," another counselor commended. "We are

recruiting men who will watch over and defend those entrusted to their protection."

"That's me, Sire. I'll defend the crown, the palace, and Christana," the young man replied.

"I will, too," the qualifying recruits said in agreement.

"On behalf of the Kingdom of Christana, thank you," another counselor acknowledged. "Training will begin Monday. Be here at first light at the horse gate. There are several skills to be learned or refined, the proper use of armaments with and without riding horseback."

The Head Counselor walked over to the applicant that came back to ask a question. Putting his hand on the young man's shoulder, he said, "You'll like working here at the palace. The royal family are good sovereigns and have great respect for the guards who vow to serve and protect."

The young man's eyes lit up. "I got the job? Thank you. You'll not be disappointed."

The new recruits thanked the counselors one more time for the opportunity to work in the palace. They left through the horse gate talking to each other. Monday seemed so far away.

Chapter 20

Sweet Treats

His tired eyes gleamed as he graded Magnus' exam. "The Lord's hand is on these brothers," the Herrgott professor noted. "Their lack of formal training and having to learn our language has not hindered them. They're at the top of the class."

"Unfortunately, their time with us is soon coming to an end. I'm grateful that I had an opportunity to have them in my class. I will miss them," replied the head of the university while grading his papers.

"Maybe one of them will return to teach here," the first professor said. Turning his head, the sound of the evening bells caught his attention. "Time for vespers."

"Let's include the brothers in our prayers tonight," the rector suggested, laying down his papers. "Maybe, the Lord has a plan for their lives that is different than what they see."

* * *

The ministerial students enjoyed walking around Herrgott. Their distinguished clothing stood out, and the local citizens recognized them. Ivar enjoyed these walks, too. Several of the citizens knew him from church services. Some of the residents had talked to him personally about needing prayer. One thankful family brought him sweet treats, a token of their appreciation. Ivar shared the baked goods with the other students. Usually, the mother of the family brought the basket of goods, but on his walk through the town this day, it was her daughter who delivered them.

A slight breeze pushed Petra's waist length hair over the side of her face. She reached up with her free hand and swept back her golden locks revealing her soft blue eyes and fair complexion.

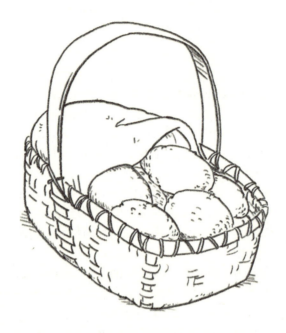

"Thank you, Petra." Ivar took the basket, offering a warm smile in return. "Where's your mother today?"

"She's not feeling well and asked me to bring the basket to you."

"Would you like for me to pray with your mother?"

"You would come to our humble home?" Petra asked.

"Of course. A home does not require fancy surroundings. It requires love." When Ivar uttered those words, he felt something inside that was both odd and good at the same time. *What was that?* he wondered.

Petra smiled and guided Ivar to her home. Ivar looked around and saw how little they had: two small bedrooms and a cooking room. Remorse overwhelmed his thoughts about accepting the baskets of sweet treats. *They're sacrificing their needs to make these baked goods. Lord, how can I repay them?*

Petra led Ivar to her mother's side. Greta gasped when she saw the visitor and pulled her cover up to her neck. Her pale face gave evidence of her unknown illness. "Reverend Ivar, you shouldn't have come here. We're not worthy."

"Greta, all of God's children are worthy. He loves us all. I have come to pray with you."

"Thank you. I want to recover. I don't want to burden my family."

"Let's take this to the Lord in prayer. Jesus, we come before You and praise Your holy name. This dear woman loves You. Greta is humble of heart and puts others' needs before her own. We put our trust in You and ask for Your help in her healing. In Your name, we pray. Amen."

Greta blinked, her eyelids becoming heavier and heavier. "I want to rest now. Thank you." Greta closed her eyes one more time and went to sleep.

"Ivar, this is wonderful," Petra whispered. "Mama has been tossing and turning in pain. She could never sleep."

"She seems restful now," Ivar noted, tiptoeing out of her room. "Thank you, Lord."

Petra reached out for Ivar's hand and handed him the basket of baked goods. "Thank you for coming and thank you for your prayer."

That funny feeling returned to Ivar. He started to talk, but the words stuck in his throat. Finally, he managed to utter, "You're welcome."

Petra opened the door. Once outside, Ivar turned around and looked at the young woman. "I'll be back tomorrow to check on your mother."

A big smile spread across Petra's face, and she waved goodbye to Ivar. Ivar noticed, and he had an equally big smile on his face as he waved, too. Ivar hummed on his way back to the University, thinking about his future. "When I go back to Christana, I'll have a position waiting for me. I'll have Grandma's house to live in. Maybe Magnus will live there, too," he muttered. Thoughts of Petra suddenly filled his mind.

I wonder if Papa felt like this for Mama?

Ivar strolled down the street reminiscing about his afternoon. Nearing the University, someone spoke suddenly from behind, "I see you have been promoted to a better position, Reverend."

Cold chills ran down Ivar's spine. He spun around and saw the stranger walking away. *How long has he been watching me?* Ivar thought. *Did he see me leave Petra's house?*

The stranger continued down the street and turned the corner. Ivar watched him until he was out of sight, but his eyes stayed glued to the corner, waiting to see if the stranger would return.

As he waited, the Head Professor of the University walked by and smelled the baked goods. "What's that sweet aroma?"

"Huh?" Ivar asked absentmindedly. His concentration on the corner was broken, and he suddenly remembered the basket in his hand.

"Something smells wonderful. What is it?"

Pulling back the cloth, Ivar displayed the goods. "They're little cakes. Greta and her daughter made them. Would you like to have one?"

"Yes, thank you," said the professor, and he savored the flavors in his mouth. "The spice and sweetness in this is delicious. Would they be interested in selling these tasty treats to the University on a regular basis? This would be a delicious addition to our meals."

"I'll ask when I see them tomorrow. Would you like to share these with the other faculty members?"

"Yes, they'll want to sample them, too." He grinned and took the basket.

* * *

Ivar raised his hand and knocked on the door. When the door opened, his eyes opened wide in astonishment. Petra's mother stood framed in the doorway. Her neatly penned back graying hair revealed her rosy cheeks and a welcoming smile.

"Good evening, Greta. I'm here to pray for you."

"Thank you, Ivar, and do come in," Greta replied. "We can offer a prayer of thanksgiving to the Lord. I feel so much better."

Ivar looked around the room and saw Petra standing by the fireplace and stirring the food in the kettle. Her eyes twinkled. At the same time, the front door opened again, and Petra's father walked in. His tanned skin indicated long hours of working outside.

"I brought you some more honey, my dear," he told his wife. Looking up, he saw a guest in his home and unconsciously raised his hands to pat down his unruly graying hair.

"Thank you, I'll need this for future baking. Tobias, this is the young man who prayed for me, Ivar."

A smile flooded Tobias' face and his eyes sparkled. He walked over to Ivar and vigorously shook his hand. "Thank you, Reverend Ivar, for your prayer. I'm thankful for you and the Lord's help. Please join us for our evening meal."

Before Ivar could speak, he watched Petra pull an extra plate off the shelf and lay it on the table. "I'd be honored, Sir."

After they started eating, Ivar told Greta about the head minister's interest in her small cakes. "He wants to know if you could bake some for the University."

"Yes, how many cakes a week would be needed?" Greta asked.

"I'll ask and bring you the information tomorrow," Ivar replied, grateful to have a reason to come back.

Tobias watched his daughter out of the corner of his eye and leaned back in his chair. "Ivar, is this your last year at the University?"

"Yes, my last year."

"Where will you go after graduation?"

"Christana."

"What if there was a position here? Would you take it?"

Tobias pressed.

Everyone straightened and looked at Ivar.

"I—I…" Ivar stuttered. He swallowed. "I'd need to pray about it."

With that response, the family slumped in their seats and sighed.

Suddenly, Ivar remembered the stranger. The hair on his arms stood up. Would that man be a danger to him or to Petra? *Stop!* he said to himself. *One step at a time.*

Ivar offered a reason for returning. "My brother is waiting for me in Christana to perform his marriage ceremony."

Noticing his daughter's frown, Tobias said, "I've heard of this kingdom. I'd like to visit Christana someday."

Petra's eyes regained their sparkle. *There's always hope,* she thought.

After eating, Ivar offered his thanks and bade the family farewell. Walking into his dormitory room, Ivar hummed a happy tune. Magnus tilted his head and greeted him, "You have it bad."

"Have what bad, Magnus?" Ivar asked.

"You know. Does she have pretty eyes?" Magnus inquired trying not to grin.

"Does it show that much?"

"Let's put it this way. I have always wanted a sister. When Johann is married, I'll get one. Now, it looks like I'll have two sisters in the future. Since Tea doesn't have a sister, she'll get one, too. Did you think those little cakes were for your great singing talent?"

"What about you, Magnus?" Ivar came right back at him.

"I've not met anyone. I'm here to study God's Word."

"I'm here for the same reason."

"Ivar, the Lord's first miracle was at a wedding," Magnus reminded his brother. "Jesus loves love."

"She is beautiful and has pretty blue eyes with golden hair," Ivar said with a big sigh.

"She sounds like Mama," Magnus reminisced. "I can still

see her face. Can you?"

"Yes, Petra is as pretty as Mama. Papa will like her. When we leave, I think her father is going to visit Christana with his family. She's an only child. If she had a sister, I would introduce you."

Magnus picked up his pillow and threw it at Ivar. "I'll find my own intended. Remember, I'm your older brother."

"Only by a few minutes!" Ivar reminded him. "Let's get some sleep. We have class in the morning."

Chapter 21

Graduation

He held the dusty pouch close to his chest as he approached the palace. The escort of guards ushered the courier through the gates. An attending servant waited and watched out of the corner of his eye as the courier tried to tidy up. Dust floated in the air each time he patted his jacket and trousers. Satisfied with his feeble attempt, the courier followed the servant and delivered his letters.

Albert rubbed his fingers over the raised wax of one of the letters. King Stefan's seal remained unbroken. Noticing Johann's name on one of the other unsealed letters, Albert held it up. "This one is for you, Johann."

Johann's fingers quickly unfolded the letter. His thoughtful smile disappeared. Albert sensed trouble. "If you need help, Johann, I'm here."

"Albert, my brothers are graduating in a few weeks. They want father and me to be there for the ceremony. I know the trip would be dangerous for both of us. Perhaps my father will be safe if he attends. I'll see them when they return to Christana." Johann stared out the window envisioning his brothers.

"Johann, let me ponder on the safety issues. Wait before you tell your father. Maybe there's a way for safe travel for everyone. In the meantime, you and Tea can finish your wedding preparations."

"Yes. The years went by so quickly. Albert, what was it like when you got married?"

"My early life with Maria was similar to yours with Tea. I

lived with Maria and her father for several years in their large palace. When we united our lives with marriage, it was the most loving and fulfilling moment. As time went by, our love grew stronger and fuller."

"I pray I will be a good husband, like you, for Tea. I want her to be happy, fulfilled, and loved. I want her to succeed in what she likes to do. I watch her with the children. Her patience, encouragement, and creativity help the little ones master the skills of reading."

"Johann, you and Tea will have a good marriage—a marriage that will endure the trials that come in life. You have overcome many trials already because of your love for God and family. Make Him the foundation of your marriage, and He will give you the strength to endure and prevail."

"Thank you, Albert. Please do me a favor."

"What's that, Johann?"

"Don't step down anytime soon."

"Let me think about it first. I could use some time off," Albert replied with a grin. "Right now, I want to go for a walk and think about your letter."

Albert headed for the courtyard. The sun shone brightly, forcing him to avert his eyes. When a guard walked up, he squinted to determine who it was. "That's it," King Albert declared loudly.

"Pardon me, Sire?" the guard asked.

"Never mind. How may I help you?"

"The queen is looking for you."

"Thank you. Let her know I'll be there soon."

The guard nodded and returned to the library where the queen waited.

"Now I have a solution to Johann's dilemma," Albert muttered and went inside. "Maria, I'm here, my dear."

Maria's chin rested on her hand while her elbow rested on the arm of the chair. With her eyes squeezed shut, she sighed several times.

"Maria, I'm here," he repeated.

Startled, Maria looked up. "Albert, I miss my father. I want him here for our daughter's wedding. He has missed so much of her life."

"Maria, I may have a solution to help Johann go to Herrgott and for your father to come here. I'll let everyone know when it's time for them to leave."

"Thank you, Albert." She gazed lovingly into her husband's eyes.

* * *

Oscar arrived with his sons at the palace gate. He scratched his head and wondered why so many guards were going to Herrgott. *Well, my son, you'll have a royal escort.*

Klaus beamed from ear to ear. "Goodbye, Papa. See you in two weeks." He turned to Benjamin. "Have fun taking care of the farm. Don't let the noises at night get the best of you."

"What?" Benjamin asked with his eyebrows drawn tight. "Oh, I'll be alone for the first time. Funny. I'll be thinking of you sleeping on the ground as I fluff up my pillow."

The head guard gave the signal and the other seven guards came closer. Two extra horses loaded with supplies trailed behind them. Ari's eyes roamed around looking for his son. Suddenly, he caught Johann's eye as his son winked. Ari winked back at the "new guard." Klaus recognized Johann in the disguise, but he addressed him in the same way as he did the other guards.

* * *

The sound of horse hoofs announced the approach of a large party. Gustav surveyed the group, and he opened his arms wide at the sight of Ari. Johann remained with the guards, concealing his identity, a condition of his ability to travel.

Ari examined the new structures that flanked both sides of the river. Cut stones and secured doors protected the guards and Gustav's family. *I wish I could tell Gustav about his nephew,* Ari mused, sighing. *Gunther misses him.*

After crossing the river, the group went on high alert. Every movement in the woods and every unusual sound intensified their anxiety.

The afternoon sun provided full illumination when the travelers passed the convergence of the two rivers. Scanning the top of the castle, Ari saw several guards dressed in uniforms. Each guard held a spear and stood at perfect attention. The hawk-emblazoned banner fluttered in the wind. One man dressed in different colors stood near the banner. *Could that be Falke?* Ari wondered. Cold chills returned for the first time since he had met the hawk man. Ari patted the banner that hung on the side of his saddle. Threads unraveled at the edges, and a hole appeared in the thinning material.

Crack! Thud! Everyone sat straight up in their saddles. The guards scanned the woods, looking for the origin of the sound. The path turned following the bend in the river. Up ahead, a dead tree stretched across the road. One guard dismounted and examined the base of the once mighty oak and reported his findings, "It's a fresh cut, Captain. Shall we clear it? We have two axes."

"No. We can't stop." Reaching for the saddle horn, the guard nodded in reply and remounted his horse.

Narrowing his eyes, the captain inched his hand toward the hilt of his sword gasping it firmly. His eyes scanned the thick overgrowth of the woods looking for signs of trouble. Seeing nothing unusual, he motioned for the group to move forward.

Clip clop, clip clop. The sound of horse hoofs on stones perked up the company's ears. Faint voices drifted down the path. The trees gave way to the sight of Herrgott. The guards headed for the palace, including Johann. Ari and Klaus secured lodging for the night at the local inn. Klaus remained at the inn while Ari ventured into the street to find his sons.

Ari paced the floor in the main hall of the University. Footsteps echoed in a hallway, and Ari turned around. He blinked his eyes to clear his vision. In the last five years, his thin-framed sons had matured into robust men.

"Father, we're so happy to see you," said Magnus.

"We've been praying for your safe journey, Father," Ivar added.

"I'm overjoyed to see you two. I'll have all my sons together again." He examined his twins closely. *They both called me Father. They're not boys anymore, but they'll always be my sons.*

"Did Johann come?" Magnus asked.

Ari carefully responded, "He's here in spirit."

Magnus and Ivar momentarily dropped their smiles. They each took an arm of their father and guided him around the University. A faculty member greeted them in Herrgott's language. When Ari replied in the same language, the twins cocked their heads and stared at their father.

"You're not the only ones who has been going to school," he shared with a grin.

Magnus and Ivar accompanied their father to the inn where they joined Klaus for the rest of the day. The bells rang, beckoning the twins for their final evening of vespers.

Ivar stood up. "When you see us tomorrow, we'll be ministers."

"And we'll be packed and ready to go home," Magnus added.

Ari noticed the melancholy expression on Ivar's face. Magnus noticed, too, patting his brother on the back. "She has pretty eyes, Papa."

Ari stared at Ivar, but the young man never said a word. Ari offered an encouraging smile which caused Ivar to smile in return. Magnus grabbed his brother's arm. "Vespers, Ivar. We have to go."

After the brothers left, Klaus asked, "Ari, do you think you'll ever return to Herrgott?"

"That's a good question, Klaus. When you are following the Lord, you never know where He might lead you."

"I find this city interesting. When I hear you practicing your vocabulary list, I repeat them to myself. I can understand some of the people here. It's empowering to be able to communicate in two languages. I want to learn more. If I lived here, I would learn the language faster."

"You have your whole life ahead of you, Klaus," Ari noted. "The more you learn, the more valuable you are to others for employment. I wouldn't want to lose you taking care of my farm, but I would never hold you back, either."

"Ari," Klaus said, pausing for a moment, "do you think I could work with the king's special breed of horses, the

Edelrosses?"

Ari looked kindly at Klaus. "If there's an opening, you'll be my first recommendation."

Satisfied with that answer, Klaus rubbed his eyes. "A bed. We can sleep in a bed tonight. I'm not fond of sleeping on the ground."

"Don't get too excited. We leave after the ceremonies tomorrow."

* * *

Johann tried to be inconspicuous, but his head bobbled back and forth. He had heard many stories about Herrgott, but the actual city surpassed his imagination. The buildings stood taller than what he was used to and the king's palace surpassed Christana's.

Stopping in front of the palace, the captain of the guard presented a letter with King Albert's wax seal. Johann knew the letter would reveal to King Stefan that he was one of the guards and craved an audience. He hoped the king would understand the gravity of the situation. The Christanan guards waited outside the gate for approval to enter. After a few moments, the Herrgott guards stepped aside and allowed the foreign guards to pass.

The Christanan guards had ridden black or brown horses, but Johann's horse had one distinguished characteristic, a white sock on each leg. This was the sign Stefan looked for as he peered out his window facing the courtyard. The king summoned his guard. "See that guard over there? Bring him to me."

"As you wish, Sire."

Stefan breathed deeply as he waited for Johann to appear. Emotions bubbled inside. He was excited to see his granddaughter's betrothed and sorrowful that he hasn't seen his family in a long time.

When the king saw Johann, he ordered everyone to leave.

His personal guard scrutinized the foreigner from head to toe and stood his ground. Johann met his eyes relaying that there was nothing for fear. He removed his sword from its scabbard and offered it to the guard. Gritting his teeth, the guard took the sword and begrudgingly left.

Stefan walked over to Johann with open arms. He momentarily stood back, looked at Johann, and then stepped forward to hug him again. "My Tea has chosen well. I want to see you two married, but if I left with you, I would likely jeopardize your journey home." That wasn't the real reason, but Stefan kept the truth to himself. He wanted to protect his kingdom and not infuriate the hawk man.

"Is it because of the hawk man?" Johann asked. "Why would he want to hurt you? He seems to torment defenseless people."

Stefan guarded his answer. "He is a tormentor, and tormentors are unpredictable. We must be careful."

"Why can't he be stopped?"

"That's a difficult question. I wish a had an easy answer." Stefan hung his head.

Johann sensed he shouldn't continue the conversation. He remembered the fallen tree and informed Stefan that the path was blocked for wagons. "I'll send an attachment of guards to have it removed immediately."

* * *

One curly lock refused to stay down. Ari tried combing it again as he glared in the mirror. *I wonder if the girl with the "pretty eyes" will be there.* Giving up on the curl, Ari walked out the door. Two of Christana's guards waited outside the inn and joined him in his walk to the University.

Crowds of people attended the ceremony. Ari straightened up and puffed his chest out when his sons received their diplomas. With parchment in hand, Magnus and Ivar eagerly sought for their father. Spotting him, they ran to his side, knocking down one of the guards. Both reached down to help him up, but the guard kept his head down and would not take their hands. Magnus bent down and asked, "Are you all right?"

"I am now," the guard replied lifting his head to look into Magnus' eyes. Johann quickly placed his finger over his lips to make the quiet sign. "I'm here in spirit," Johann said, winking at them.

Magnus and Ivar instinctively knew they would have to treat him as a guard until they were told otherwise. Once they helped the "guard" up, they collided into another person. When Magnus turned around to see who he had bumped this time, he saw a young woman with pretty eyes. Then he noticed Ivar's eyes lightening up.

"Hello," Magnus said. "Ivar has told me so much about you."

Normally, Ivar would have chided his brother, but he let it pass. "Father," Ivar said smiling broadly, "this is Petra."

Petra didn't understand the words Ivar used, because he talked in the language of Christana. But she knew it was an introduction and replied, "Hello, Sir."

Ari greeted Petra in her language, "Hello, Petra. I'm pleased to meet you."

"Ivar!" Petra exclaimed. "Your father knows my language."

"Just a little," Ari informed her.

Ivar looked at Johann and talked to him with his eyes: *I'm so thankful you're here, but I can't include you right now.* Johann pursed his lips and nodded.

Petra's parents finally caught up with their daughter. "Our Petra can run as fast as a horse," Tobias said. "I'm Tobias and this is my wife, Greta."

Ari shook both of their hands and talked to them a little in their native language. Magnus and Ivar marveled at how much their father had learned.

"We won't be able to tell secrets around you in the Herrgott language," Magnus said. "Let's let Ivar and Petra finish their goodbyes. I'll go get our belongings. I'll need help. Guard, could you come with me?"

The guard nodded and followed Magnus to his quarters. Once they were alone, Johann hugged his brother. "I'm so proud of you and Ivar. As you can see, we must be careful. Albert is concerned about our safety. We must leave quickly. The rest of the guards are waiting for us. You cannot acknowledge me until we are back at the palace in Christana. We never know who can be trusted or who is watching." The brothers picked up the baggage and headed for the horses.

Magnus found Ivar and Petra still talking. Greta handed Ivar a large basket of baked cakes. The delicious aroma drifted in Johann's direction, and he turned around. *Yum*, he thought as his mouth watered.

"It's time, Ivar," Magnus said sadly. "I hope you can come to our town someday, Petra. When you do, bring some baked treats."

Petra smiled. She turned to Ivar, looked into his eyes, and hugged him. Ivar almost went limp. Any second thoughts about his feelings for Petra vanished. He gave her a little kiss on the cheek and told her goodbye one more time.

Tears rolled down Petra's face. Her parents stood by her side, and they all waved goodbye. Magnus saw tears in Ivar's eyes, but he never said a word. He put his arm around his bother and walked him to the horses.

"Need help with that robe?" Magnus asked. Ivar threw his brother an odd look. "Riding may be more comfortable if you took it off."

Ivar looked down and quietly removed his robe. *Home. In a few days, I'll be home. I have lived in this town for five years. I'll miss it.*

Chapter 22

Homecoming

The earthy smell of fresh cut wood permeated the air. About half of the fallen tree had been removed. The caravan of guards and their charges rode quietly by, wondering who chopped it down and why.

The Christanan guards displayed an assertive posture that provided a secure atmosphere for Ari's group. In passing Falke's castle, they saw several guards standing at attention on the ramparts, but no sign of the hawk man.

Maybe he's bored with us, Ari thought. He looked forward and noticed that all three of his sons happened to be riding side by side. *Thank you, Jesus. Without You, none of this would be possible.*

The lengthy trip offered Johann plenty of opportunities to reflect on his experience being a guard. He had respect for the men in uniform, but roleplaying a guard gave him a deeper appreciation of the loyalty guards have for the crown. "It's not a calling for everyone," Johann muttered. "In the future, I'll be more involved in the recruiting progress."

* * *

News of the guards' arrival brought the royal family to the courtyard. Maria scanned the group. "Where's my father?" Johann looked at her and slowly shook his head. Maria subtly bit her lower lip. Tears welled in her eyes. Albert wrapped his arm around her shoulder and comforted his wife.

Tea almost knocked Johann down when the weary "guard" walked toward her. Johann wrapped his arms around her waist, lifted her off her feet, and twirled her in a circle. After he lowered her back to the ground, Tea grabbed Johann's hand and guided him to a quiet place to talk.

Later on, Johann thought about the next day. *I'll be with my brothers at the farm tomorrow. The whole family together again. Thank You, Lord.*

* * *

On the way home, Ari's group passed the church. Sitting outside on the church step, Lars looked up and waved. Magnus and Ivar quickly dismounted and ran up to Lars. Both brothers embraced him. "What do I owe this privilege?" Lars asked, smiling broadly.

"If it hadn't been for you," Magnus said, "we wouldn't have become ministers."

"I thank you for the compliment," Lars began, "but the arm of the Lord is not too short to accomplish His ways. If it wasn't me, it would be someone else. Now that you are back, can I step down?"

"And we were concerned about taking your position away," Ivar humbly responded.

"Did either of you learn how to play the organ?" Lars asked.

"No." Magnus replied.

"Good!" Lars quipped. "I have a job as the organist. I love to play anyway. I'll teach your children to play, too."

"Lars," Ivar interjected, "we're not married."

"Yet," Magnus threw in.

Lars looked at Magnus. Magnus shook his head and pointed to Ivar. Ivar turned his head and looked the other way.

"Sounds like we'll have two weddings to plan for," Lars said with a cute grin.

Ari listened to those words. He remembered the time his mother-by-marriage, Elina, said those very words about him and her daughter. *Johanna,* Ari mused, *I can say your name and not be sad or angry that you're gone. I get to keep our love even though you're with the Lord.*

While Ari waved goodbye to Lars, he caught a glimpse of a man wearing a hooded cloak turning his face away. He glanced over to his sons, but they were looking in the opposite direction. Returning his attention for the hooded man Ari watched him walk away.

"Two weddings?" the hooded man muttered kicking the dirt.

Benjamin heard the noisy travelers when they entered the yard and walked outside. "Welcome back. As soon as everyone settles in, I'll return home."

"Benjamin," Ari said, "go home to your family. We'll take care of it."

Klaus looked at Ari and his sons. "If you don't mind, I want to see my parents."

Ari waved them both goodbye. The remaining three men sat at the table. Ari's hands rested on the table as he admired his sons then lowered his head and wept. Magnus and Ivar tried to console him, but Ari shook his head. "Sons, I'm not sad. I'm overwhelmed. I'm thankful. All of my sons are serving the Lord. I don't understand why your mother had to go so early in her life, but the Lord worked for good in this terrible circumstance. The Lord has forgiven this wretched creature of his sins and has blessed me."

"Papa," Magnus began, "Paul wrote a letter to the Christians in Rome and told them, 'We know that God works for good in all things for those who love Him and are called according to His purpose.' Loosely, that means God makes something good out of something terrible. Mama's passing was terrible, but good things have happened."

"Just think," Ivar added. "Johann wouldn't be our future king, and we wouldn't be ministers."

"Thank you. You make these words easy to understand. I still miss your mother. One day, I'll see her again, but not today."

"Papa," Ivar said looking admiringly into his father's eyes, "you can talk about Mama now. We have never heard you talk about Mama since she died."

Ari placed his hand on top of the locket under his shirt. "I thank the Lord for that ability. I'd be lost without Him." A sudden thought entered Ari's mind and he changed the subject. "Sons, we have a wedding coming soon. Are you two ready to get a sister?"

"Maybe two," Magnus threw in.

"First things first, Brother," Ivar retorted. "It's been a week since we slept in a bed, and tonight we get to sleep in our own beds!"

"Well said," Ari pointed out. "Let's turn in for the night. Tomorrow will be here in a few hours, and we'll have a busy day. Good night, sons. God bless you, and welcome home."

The next morning, Ari woke up before his sons. He looked outside and noticed that Benjamin and Klaus had not yet arrived. "I didn't oversleep. This is going to be a wonderful day!"

Ivar came out of the bedroom first. He appreciated the opportunity to talk to his father alone. "Let's go outside, Papa." Walking to the barn, Ivar asked, "Who is going to stay with you, Papa?"

"What do you mean?"

"It's time to use Grandma's cottage. Magnus and I are here, and Klaus has been living with you. Where do you suggest everyone should stay?"

"Ivar, are you planning to stay in Christana or Herrgott?"

Ivar looked at his father with wide eyes. He paused before he replied. "Papa, I have strong feelings for Petra. I'm here, but part of me is there."

"It's called love, Son." Ari put his arm around Ivar's shoulder. "If the feeling never leaves you, then, you have a decision to make. Let the Lord's peace be your compass. Either way, I'll support you." Contemplating his father's words, Ivar looked at him in silence.

Ari's thoughts drifted to the time when he had fallen in love with Johanna. *Thank You, my Heavenly Father,* he silently prayed. *I trust in You for wisdom to be a good father for my sons. As You know, we have to tell them what they need to hear, not what they want to hear.* Ari could almost feel the Lord putting His arm around his shoulders.

Klaus and Benjamin rode in and waved. "Ari," Benjamin yelled, "you must be feeling better." Ari threw him a puzzled look. "You're up before we got here."

Ivar gave his father an odd look. "Don't ask," Ari requested, and he walked over to the approaching brothers. "How's your family?" Ari asked.

"Mama and Papa are fine," Klaus replied. "But Mama has reorganized my room into something else. Do you think she's sending me a message?"

Ivar looked at his father. Slightly lowering his chin, he glanced up, and gave him "the look."

"Okay, okay," Ari surrendered.

"Okay, what?" Benjamin asked.

"Okay, for who stays where," Ari replied.

Klaus turned pale. All eyes focused on Ari.

"Ivar," Ari began, "I love you dearly, but it's time you lived in your own home. You'll have to share with Magnus."

"Share what?" Magnus asked as he walked toward the group.

"It's about time you woke up," Ari continued. "You and your brother are grown men. You two need to have your own home, but you'll have to share your grandmother's cottage."

"Yes!" Magnus replied, "I finally get a room to myself. Ivar, you want the top room or first floor?"

Ivar shrugged.

Klaus remained quiet when Ari looked at him. "Your room is still available, if you want it."

"I can stay?" Klaus asked.

"Of course," Ari replied. "Your things are still there waiting for you. Men, let's go eat. If Johann doesn't hurry up, he'll get clean up duty."

"Papa!" Magnus and Ivar said simultaneously.

"Exactly! I'm Papa," Ari affirmed with a big grin. "So, he better hurry up."

Johann came around the lane as the others headed for the house.

"Last one in cleans up," yelled Magnus.

Johann raced his mount to the house and leaped off the horse pulling the horse's reins as he ran to the rail.

"Not fair," Ivar yelled. "You had an advantage."

"Fair!" yelled Johann. "You made rules before I got here."

"Ari is bringing up the rear," Benjamin added.

Ari, more than satisfied to watch all his "boys" running to the house, walked to the door.

When he entered the cooking room, the two sets of brothers laughed and teased each other. *Johanna,* Ari thought, *our home is full of love.*

Ivar picked up Johann's hand, examined it, and said, "Your hands look a little rough. Are those books you study heavy to pick up?"

Johann picked up Ivar's hand and examined it. "Just about as heavy as that basketful of sweet treats," he replied with a big grin. Magnus decided to wait until they got outside to share his banter with Johann, so he kept quiet.

Everyone pitched in and helped clean up. Ari picked up the Bible and opened it. Magnus and Ivar stopped their work and sat next to their father. Johann joined them. Benjamin and Klaus stopped working and stood by the fireplace.

Ari let the Bible fall open to a page of its own choosing, the book of Johann (John), the fifteenth chapter. Ari read it aloud, "Greater love has no one than this, that he lay down his life for his friends."

Quietness blanketed the room. Even the wind ceased to blow. Ivar stood up and interrupted the silence. "Jesus did this for us. He died to pay the price of our sins and His resurrection conquered death. When we believe in Him and ask Him into our lives, we are united with God the Father, Son and Holy Spirit. His death, gives us life, eternal life, and nothing can take it away from us."

"Johann," Magnus added, "you know the disciple Jesus loved the most was Johann (John)."

"I can tell you who I love the most," Ari stated. All eyes fixated on him now. "The first one who will name their firstborn after me."

Johann grinned. Ivar and Magnus crossed their arms and frowned. "Unfair," Ivar quipped.

"Fair, so get busy, Ivar," Johann teased.

"Johann," Magnus calmly added, "what if your firstborn is a girl? Will she be so understanding with that name?"

Benjamin and Klaus couldn't hold it in any longer. Their faces turned red as they looked at each other and broke out in laugher. Ivar, Magnus, and Johann joined them. Ari calmly closed the Bible, placed it back on the shelf, and walked out the door. As he strolled to the barn, he held up both of his arms and said in a loud voice, "The Lord is my banner!"

Walking to the barn, Johann shared his thoughts about the scripture. "When I was pretending to be a guard, I knew every guard would protect me and everyone in our group. Not because they loved us so much. It was because they had made a decision. Jesus loves us, *and* He made a decision to follow the Father's will even though it would cost Him His life."

Klaus asked, "Benjamin, would you do that, die for people

you don't know?"

"A man doesn't know what he'll do until he is put in that position, but this I know for sure. When it comes to family and friends, I'll defend them. I'd give my life, so they may live."

Silence surrounded them until they reached the corral. Watching Ari ready a horse, Benjamin spoke up, "Come on guys, I want to see Johann fall on his, uh, royal bottom again!"

Magnus and Ivar cocked an eyebrow at their brother with a bewildered look. "Benjamin," Johann replied, "it's your turn today."

At the end of the workday, Johann and Benjamin returned to their homes in town. At sunset, Ivar and Magnus walked over to their grandmother's cottage. Fresh food lay on the cooking room table, and neatly stacked wood filled the fireplace. A note rested on the table.

Magnus and Ivar,

Welcome home. This cottage has been empty too long. I hope you will settle in and come see me at the church in the morning.

Lars

"We are blessed, Ivar," Magnus said.

"Yes, we are," Ivar agreed.

"Since you don't care, I'll take the first-floor bedroom," Magnus proclaimed and walked into the room.

"It's all yours, Magnus." Thinking of Petra, he whispered,

"I may not be here long anyway. I'll write her a letter tonight."

Chapter 23

On One Condition

The quietness startled Magnus. *Where's Ivar?* He looked around for his brother before remembering. "He's upstairs." Although he had been elated to have his own room, it felt odd to be separated.

In the solitude of the cooking room, Ivar sat with folded hands offering his morning prayers to the Lord. The noise of Magnus' shuffling feet brought the personal devotion to an end.

"Good morning, Ivar. Are you ready to start work today?"

Ivar scratched his head as he looked around. "Ready, but we have to fix our own food. What do I do first?"

Magnus gave his brother the oddest look. "Didn't we have this conversation a few years ago? Whatever you do, don't throw a log on the ashes."

Ivar returned his brother's odd look. A smile grew on his face. Memories of throwing a log on the ashes which caused them to fly everywhere came rolling back. When he reached for a rag to clean up the mess, the family Bible was uncovered. That began their journey to become ministers.

"Maybe just a little bit for old time's sake," Ivar quipped with a mischievous grin.

"No!" Magnus roared back. "We're meeting with Lars this morning, remember?"

"Later then?"

Magnus rolled his eyes, but Ivar wanted to enjoy every moment with his brother before one of them left to start a new home.

Lars stood on the church doorstep pretending to clean the front windows as he waited for the two brothers. "They're good men, Lord. Thank You for allowing me to be part of Your plan. Put Your hand upon me and direct me with Your Holy Spirit as I transition them into Your church. In Your name, I pray. Amen," he softly prayed. Looking up, he saw the twins. "Good morning, Reverends," Lars greeted the brothers. "Did you sleep well?"

"Yes," Ivar replied. "For the first time in our lives, we had a room to ourselves."

"Until you get married," Magnus quipped.

Lars gave Magnus one of those looks that required stern stares and pursed lips. Magnus got the point and didn't tease Ivar again. "Thank you," Ivar whispered to Lars as he walked by.

The size of the church surprised the brothers when they entered. "I remember it being bigger, but I was eight years old at the time," Ivar noted.

"It could use some improvements. We need more room for the worshipers. It's getting crowded in here," said Lars.

"Have you considered offering two services on Sunday?" Magnus asked.

"See," Lars eyes lit up, "that's what we need. Our kingdom is growing. We have to acclimate to the needs of its people. Great idea, Magnus. I'm sure you both will have many more."

Lars led the brothers to the altar. "Johann and Tea will be wanting to practice the wedding ceremony soon. Where do you suggest you two should stand?"

Magnus offered his opinion, and Ivar agreed.

"Ivar, I left my Book of Services in the office. Would you go get it for me?" Lars asked.

"Of course."

He walked in the direction Lars pointed and found the office at the end of a hallway. Ivar opened the door and saw a book laying on the desk. Turning his head, he noticed a woman standing in front of the window looking outside.

"Good morning," Ivar politely greeted her.

"Good morning," the woman replied with a slight accent in her voice.

As she turned around, Ivar suddenly noticed a familiar fragrance, a sweet aroma. It reminded him of sweet treats. "Petra!" he cried out. His eyes opened wide with surprise. His knees wobbled as he looked at her with amazement. "I'm so happy to see you."

Ivar didn't know what to do. Should he walk over to her? Could he embrace her? He didn't have to make that decision. Petra ran to him and gathered him in her arms.

Ivar took a deep breath, stepped back, picked up Petra's hands, and said, "Petra, I just wrote you a letter last night and here you are." As Petra held hands with Ivar, she turned her head toward the corner of the room. Ivar also looked. There stood two people, Tobias and Greta. Ivar immediately dropped Petra's hands.

"Good morning, Ivar," Tobias said with a hearty smile.

"Good to see you." Confusion filled Ivar's mind and he crafted an awkward expression on his face. "Ivar, Petra cried all day after you left. As her father, it broke my heart. She wanted to be near you. I told her I'd support her either way."

"My father said the same thing to me," Ivar interjected.

"King Stefan assembled a caravan that was headed for Christana the day after you left. I asked if we could join them. We were given permission to travel with the guards and merchants. We arrived yesterday."

"Were you the ones who brought the food in?" Ivar asked.

"Yes," Greta confirmed. "we didn't leave the sweet treats. That would be too much of a hint we were here. The note was Reverend Lars idea."

Ivar looked back at Petra. "Petra, I want to read my letter to you."

He opened the letter and read it out loud, "Dearest Petra, I pray you are well. Even though it has only been a week since I saw you, it feels much longer. I do not know how to put my feelings into words, but I'll try.

"Petra, I have never felt this way before meeting you. I love my father and brothers, but this feeling is different. Being separated from my family did not affect me the way being separated from you has. I feel I left part of me in Herrgott. I have a commitment to the church in Christana, but devoting my heart to my new position is difficult when part of it is with you.

"As soon as I can, with your parents' permission, I will come to see you. Please let me know when I can see you. Truly yours, Ivar."

Tobias immediately added, "You have our permission!" Greta smiled and quickly nodded.

Ivar held Petra's hand again and confessed, "Petra, I want to be able to give you your heart's desires, but I have very little to offer right now. Could you wait for me?"

"Ivar," Petra began, "I couldn't wait for you in Herrgott, but I can wait for you here."

Ivar looked at Tobias and Greta and asked, "May I?"

"Yes!" they replied.

Ivar lowered his knee to the ground. He took Petra's other hand into his hand. With tears in his eyes he asked, "Petra, will you marry me?"

"Yes, on one condition."

Petra's parents looked mortified. They quickly shook their heads.

What's the condition? Ivar asked himself. His hands trembled as he still held Petra's hands. His face turned pale. Ivar took a deep breath and asked, "What is the condition, Petra?"

"I want to teach children about the Bible just as you teach adults about the Bible. It would be a school offered on Sunday. Maybe we could call it Sunday School."

Overwhelmed by the request, Ivar slumped and sat on the floor. Now, Petra turned pale. He turned his head toward her.

"Is that all?" he asked while his natural color returned to his complexion. "Of course, you can. We'll be a team doing the Lord's work." For the first time, Ivar shared his true feelings, "I love you, Petra. With my whole heart, I love you."

"I love you. From the first time I saw you, I knew you were the one, my only true love."

Greta went limp, and Tobias caught her before she fell. "Daughter, I understand why couples need to discuss their issues in private. That was too much for us."

"Magnus must be wondering what has happened to me," Ivar said. "Lars knows, but not my brother. Let's go see them."

Magnus looked at the direction where Ivar disappeared. Lars never said a word. He continued talking about the procedures of previous weddings and asked if there were new ideas being taught at the University. Ivar entered the sanctuary first.

"It's about time you returned. Did you get lost?" Magnus teased.

Petra entered the sanctuary with her parents. Magnus

stared, Lars smiled, and Ivar announced, "Magnus, you'll have two sisters in the future. Petra and I are betrothed."

Magnus' mouth dropped opened. Finally, he came to his senses. "Welcome to the family, Petra." He walked over and gave her a brotherly hug. "Father is getting two daughters."

"We have not set a date," Ivar added. "I want to get established with our work before we wed."

"Before who weds?" Johann asked as he walked into the church with his father.

Ivar gazed affectionately into Petra's blue eyes. "Petra and I are betrothed."

"Welcome to the family," Ari proclaimed. "Now, I have two daughters. Tobias and Greta, you have a son."

"We always wanted a son," Greta shared. "We knew the Lord would provide."

Ari and his sons all looked at each other and gave the thumbs up gesture, a sign of approval, like they did in the days of the gladiators. Simultaneously, Ari, Johann, and Ivar looked at Magnus. "No, no, not yet," Magnus said emphatically.

"I have a cousin," Petra offered. "She has pretty eyes." Everyone laughed except Petra. Frowning, Petra repeated, "She does have pretty eyes."

"Petra," Magus began, "how long are you and your parents staying in Christana?"

Petra didn't know how to truthfully answer the question, so her father did. "We're all staying until the royal wedding," Tobias started. "Then, Greta and I will return to Herrgott."

"Petra, will you be staying by yourself?" Magnus asked.

"Yes, I'll look for a place to stay this week, perhaps at the inn. I can cook and bake to earn my wages."

Magnus looked at Ivar. Ivar nodded. "All of you are welcome to stay at our cottage. Tobias, Greta, we'll watch over her when you leave. Petra, you can stay there as long as you want."

Petra's eyes filled with tears. Her new family would be her protectors.

"I would like to offer another plan for you to choose from," Ari interjected. All eyes focused on him now. "How about all the boys, I mean men, stay at the cottage, and you, Petra, stay at my house."

Petra looked at the brothers. They all nodded. Petra looked at her parents. They nodded. "Yes," she agreed. "On one condition."

Again? Ivar thought.

"I get to cook for everyone," she quickly replied. "I hear you could use a good cook." Ari gave Ivar an odd look. Ivar, Tobias, and Greta let out a huge sigh of relief.

Magnus smiled and said, "On one condition." Now, the eyes focused on him. "Ivar, the bottom bedroom is big enough. We can put up a dividing wall and add another entrance. Klaus can sleep upstairs."

"Perfect!" Ivar agreed. "You still get a room to yourself."

Chapter 24

Royal Wedding

The candle flames flickered when Johann walked by. He pressed his hand on his gut, hoping to calm the butterflies fluttering in his stomach. "Father, I'm a little nervous. Did you feel this way when you married Mama?"

"Yes, Son," Ari replied. "But I kept my eye on the goal."

"Goal?"

"My goal was to make your mother the happiest woman in Christana. My thoughts focused on her."

"Papa, what would I do without you? You're a good father."

Ari grasped Johann's upper arms. "Son, I'm here for you just as our Heavenly Father is here for us. You'll be a good husband and father. I'm proud of you, Son."

The knock on the door echoed in the room, and a voice announced, "It's time."

Cheers and applause filled the town square when Johann exited the palace. Several guards stood at attention and had formed a perimeter from the palace to the church entrance. Waving to the crowd, Johann realized that his butterflies had departed but his heart pounded harder with each step he took. He barely felt his father's arm laying across his shoulders.

Ari scanned the crowd of smiling faces. His eyes caught a glimpse of a scowl on a man's face standing between two guards. Tangled brown hair partially covered the face of this man of small stature, but his beady black eyes sent a quick chill into Ari's spirit. Ari quickly faced Johann to see if his son had noticed the man, but Johann's eyes were focused on the church.

When Ari looked back, the man was gone.

Johann paused at the church doorway and offered a quiet prayer. Looking inside, he scanned the people sitting in the pews, family, friends, royal court members, and lots of children.

"The children outnumber the adults," Johann told his father. "We couldn't include everyone in town, so Tea and I decided to just invite the school children."

Ari chuckled.

Magnus and Ivar took their positions. When Johann reached the altar, Magnus greeted his brother, "Prince Johann, you look stunning." The children giggled. Johann grinned and relaxed a little.

Silence expanded over the sanctuary. The doors opened and Lars started the organ music. In walked Princess Dorothea with her father on one side and her mother on her other.

A smile spread across Ari's face when he saw Tea. Magnus' and Ivar's eyes welled up with tears. Johann's mouth dropped open when he saw Tea and her dress. "Blue, Mama's dress was blue."

Tea had asked Ari if he still had any dresses of his Johanna. Only one dress remained: the dress Johanna had worn the day she collapsed to the floor and died in his arms with his sons by his side. Tea wanted Johanna to be part of the wedding and had asked Ari if she could wear the dress. Only Tea, her parents, and Ari knew. Johanna was remembered, in spirit, at her son's wedding.

"Thank you," Johann quietly mouthed to Tea.

Ivar handed Johann a handkerchief to wipe his face. He managed to find a dry spot.

"Are you ready, Johann?" Ivar asked.

"Yes."

Ivar nodded to the royal family. As they walked, Tea looked at the only decorations around the church. Yellow flowers, tucked in white bows, graced the ends of the pews and the altar.

Albert wiped his clammy palms on his jacket; Maria fought

to keep her tears in check, but Tea beamed all the way down the aisle. Reaching the altar, Magnus asked, "Who gives this woman to be married?"

King Albert replied, "Her mother and I." Albert took his daughter's hand and placed it in Johann's hand. Afterward, he and Maria joined Ari in the front pew. Benjamin and Meta sat in the front row on the other side with Klaus and his parents. Petra and her parents sat behind the royal family.

During the vows, Maria sighed deeply. *I wish my father could be here today.* She briefly thought about the man living in the castle and shuttered.

At the end of the ceremony, Ivar announced, "I pronounce you husband and wife. God bless your marriage. You may kiss your bride."

Magnus leaned over and whispered to Ivar, "Husband and wife? I thought it was man and wife."

"Only the woman gets married?" Ivar quipped. "I made sure they were both married."

Johann extended his hand to Tea. She placed her hand in his and they turned toward their parents. Albert nodded, Maria dabbed a tear, and Ari patted his locket under his shirt. The quiet moment only lasted a few seconds.

Lars pressed down on the keys of the organ and everyone stood up. Joyful cheers erupted all over the church with the children's voices drowning out the adults. Johann and Tea strolled down the aisle nodding to their guests.

When the attendants opened the doors, the church bells rang out announcing the wedding couple. Johann and Tea paused on the church steps and waved to the crowd. Shouts of joy and praise flowed through the multitude of people gathered in the town square. Some of the spectators had banners that they waved back and forth. Some had flower petals that they tossed on the ground for the newlyweds to walk on.

The wedding guests accompanied the royal family to the palace courtyard. The children followed while their parents patiently waited in the square.

Flowers, ribbons, and banners decorated the courtyard. Soft stringed music floated through the air. Servants dressed in their formal attire attended their guests.

Sweet aromas surrounded the platters of tasty treats that rested on the tables. Low throated "mms" followed as the children tasted a little cake that looked like a child. Some children nibbled the feet first, some nibble the hands first, and some just bit the head off with one bite.

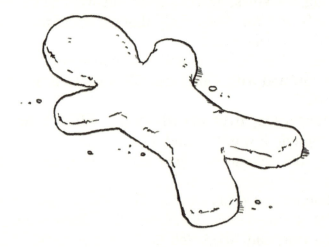

"Very good," Albert said admiring his legless treat. "You're a great baker."

"Thank you," said Greta. "But, I did have help. Benjamin carved out a dough cutter. All the shapes are the same."

"That's good to know. I may want Benjamin to carve me something someday," Albert said and finished his treat.

Chapter 25

Replacement

Toward the end of summer, Tea began preparing for her new group of students, but when, one day, she woke up not feeling very well, all thoughts of her upcoming classes fled her mind. Johann called for the Court Physician who made Johann stay in the hall during the examination. Albert and Maria smiled knowingly, but not Johann. Worry filled his heart, and he quietly prayed, "Jesus, be with my Tea. Keep her out of harm's way. In Your name, I pray. Amen."

A few moments later the doors opened. The physician

asked for Johann to come in. Albert and Maria stood up and started for the door, too, but the Court Physician put his hand up and stopped them. He quietly shut the doors behind Johann. Now, Albert and Maria looked worried.

Tea noticed the concerned look on Johann's face. She pointed to her own face and smiled broadly. Folding her arms, she grabbed her elbows and rocked her arms back and forth. Johann's face lit up, and he yelled, "A baby!"

Immediately, Albert sprang to his feet and headed for the door. Maria grabbed his arm and shook her head. He reluctantly shuffled back to his chair.

"Tea," Johann asked. "How are you feeling?"

"A little sick to my stomach and exhausted."

Thoughts of his own mother and how her body became weakened over time alarmed Johann. Tea sensed it. "Johann, I'll be just fine. I'm not going anywhere."

Johann leaned over and grasped her in his arms, "Tea, I now see what my father went through. I'm not as strong as he is. We have to keep you safe. Please, be careful."

"Johann, I promise. Let's straighten up and let my parents in. I'm sure they heard you in the hall. I'm surprised Papa hasn't come in already."

The Court Physician remembered treating Johanna years ago. "Johann, medicine has improved since your mother's passing. Just to be on the safe side, I'll call for one of my colleagues to assist me for the next few months."

"Thank you. Whatever you need, you will have it." The physician nodded and went to the doors.

Staring at the rug, Albert paced the floor wringing his hands. The doors creaked open. He looked up and saw the physician smiling. Albert took Maria's hand and they walked to their daughter's side.

"Papa, you're a Pawpaw."

Albert raised his arms up in the air and exclaimed, "Praises to You, my Lord!"

Maria gazed at her husband. Admiration filled her heart.

Turning toward her daughter, she knelt down and kissed Tea on the cheek. "Congratulations, sweetheart." Maria stood back up. "Oh!"

"What's wrong, Mama?"

"Ma'am, we're going to need a replacement for you."

"Teaching. You're right. I cannot fulfill my role for the full year. Who are we going to get to take my place?"

"Let the counselors help with that decision," Albert said. "Right now, we're going to follow the physician's orders. She needs complete rest, right?" Albert asked, looking directly at the Court Physician.

"Yes, Sire," he quickly added, "plenty of rest."

As Albert and Maria entered the hallway, their feet barely touched the floor. Albert counted on his fingers. Maria noticed. "March or April will be our grandchild's birthday."

"What? How did you know that I was—"

Maria interrupted, "Albert, I'm a woman and a mother. I know about these things."

"I love my ladies dearly."

* * *

Later that day, Johann suggested Benjamin's wife, Meta, as a possible candidate for the teaching position. Albert liked that choice. "Let's ask Benjamin if his wife is interested."

At the evening meal, Benjamin asked Meta about the teaching position. She jumped out of her chair. "I have always wanted to teach. Our son is almost school age."

"Meta, I have watched you teaching him at home. Josef already knows how to read. He'll blend right in."

"Thank you, Benjamin."

"Why are you thanking me?"

"You're a loving and supportive husband."

"Happy wife, happy life."

Meta lowered her chin and raised her eyes upward and stared at her husband. Then, she raised her head and chuckled.

"I'm married to a schoolteacher," he teased her. "I better behave or I'll have to do extra school work."

"Silly man," Meta responded. "I wouldn't make you do that. You'd have to sit in a corner until you could tell me why your behavior was inappropriate and what your plan was to improve it."

"Like I said, I better behave."

* * *

Johann paced the floor. Soon he would share one of Albert's duties as king, holding court for the people of Christana. Determined to succeed, Johann prayed for wisdom. God heard those petitions. When it suited His timing, he answered Johann's prayers.

One day, King Albert let Johann go into the chamber alone for quiet contemplation. When Johann came out, he would rule on the case he'd heard. While Albert waited, he went over the testimony and evidence presented. He concluded in his mind what the verdict should be. Johann returned and gave his summation.

Albert nodded. "Well done. Your conclusion and presentation are better than what mine would have been."

The main doors suddenly opened. Albert and Johann looked up at the intrusion and saw a guard rushing into the room. "It's time," he blurted out.

Some of the petitioners cheered. One man smirked and glared at his opponent when he said, "Go, we'll come back later."

Afterward, the man turned pale as he realized he broke protocol addressing the king and prince without permission. But Albert and Johann both patted him on the back as they walked by. "Thank you!" they said.

By the time Albert and Johann reached Tea's room, they heard high-pitched crying. "That's not Tea," Johann declared.

Albert looked at Johann, "It's the baby!"

Maria opened the doors. Strands of her hair clung to the perspiration on her face. She had been with her daughter all day. Johann rushed to Tea. Her face glowed and her eyes sparkled. Turning his head, he looked at the baby wrapped in the blanket. A small tiara rested on the pillow. "Tiara," he blurted out. "I have a daughter!"

Maria stood by her husband and reminisced, "Those words sound familiar."

"Was I like this, too?" Albert asked.

"No, dear, you were worse."

"Papa, your granddaughter wants to see her pawpaw."

"That's right!" Albert said. "I'm a pawpaw."

Memories of Tea as a baby flooded Maria's thoughts. She lifted up her granddaughter and cradled her in her arms. Albert peeked over her shoulder. "She looks just like Tea when she was born." Maria handed the baby to Johann.

Johann's hands slightly trembled. "What if I drop her?"

"If you were holding Tea, would you drop her?" Maria asked. "This little lady is much lighter. You won't drop her."

Johann propped his daughter's head in the crook of his arm. Fatherhood immediately captured his heart. "What shall we call her?" Johann asked Tea.

"Your mother's name is Johanna. We could name her after your mother."

"You would do that for me?" Johann looked at his daughter, then, looked at Tea. "Could we call her Anna?"

"I love it," Albert blurted out.

"I do, too," Maria added.

"Of course," Tea confirmed with a sheepish grin. "That was my plan all along. I just wanted you to say it first."

A guard delivered the announcement to Ari, Magnus, and Ivar. Ari arrived first and walked quickly to Tea's side. "My little princess," he said as he gazed into the baby's blue eyes.

"Your little princess, Johanna," Johann shared.

Ari's arms turned to jelly. "Johanna? Her name is Johanna?" He raised his head. "Thank you, Lord. You have given us Johanna."

Albert walked up and said, "Let's make a gentleman's agreement. No competition about who is the best pawpaw."

"Agreed," Ari said. "Now, it's time for this pawpaw to hold his favorite granddaughter."

Magnus and Ivar walked into the room. "Uncle Magnus, Uncle Ivar, come and meet your niece, Johanna," Johann said. The uncles didn't care about the name. They just wanted to see this little bundle of joy.

"Anna, sweetie," Ivar started. "It's Uncle Ivar, the cute one."

"Hey," Magnus said with indignation, "that's not polite."

"Magnus, we're identical twins."

"All right, you're forgiven. Now, scoot over! It's my turn." Magnus started making baby sounds to little Anna.

"Tea, if you need a babysitter, I recommend Magnus," Ivar teased. Then, Ivar put his hand on Johann's back, "Well done, Brother. Well done."

Ordinarily, Magnus would have teased Ivar about being the next father, but he was too busy playing with his niece.

I wonder how pretty Petra's cousin's eyes are? Ivar contemplated. *Maybe she should come for a visit. I'll talk it over with Petra.*

Chapter 26

Family Reunion

H er ears perked up and her heart raced. Petra looked into Ivar's eyes as she clasped her hands together. Salty tears welled up and stung her eyes. "We can invite her? I haven't seen any of my family in months."

"Of course. Father said Angela is welcome to come," Ivar replied pronouncing the name as ANG-geh-la.

"I have so much to tell her."

"Tell her when she gets here. Remember, we have to be careful what we write to others."

Petra searched for the writing materials. Ink dripped from the quill as she prepared the stylus for writing. *Hmm, what is safe to say?* she pondered as she began the letter. *I'll send one to Mama, too.* She kept the letters brief and handed them to Ivar as he left for town.

Ivar carried the letters into the church. "I better read these. Thank goodness, they don't have a wax seal on them," he muttered. He unfolded the letters and read their contents. *They appear harmless,* he surmised as he folded them back up and took them to the courier.

"I leave for Herrgott tomorrow," the courier said.

"Do you ride alone?" Ivar asked.

"No, I have an escort, but I don't know why. I could ride this path in my sleep. As soon as I get to Herrgott, I come right back to Christana with new letters."

"Thank you for taking mine." Ivar watched the courier insert the letters in his pouch. "I hope he's careful," Ivar mumbled as he walked back to the church.

* * *

Tea hovered over her daughter's cradle. "You're going to spoil her," Maria said.

"She never cries when I'm around," Tea replied.

"Of course not. You pick her up before she has a chance to cry."

"Mama!" Tea protested.

"But I'm happy to see you back to your old self again. The Court Physician was right about your health."

Tea picked up a wooden rattle and shook it. Anna turned her head and watched the toy. "She likes her rattle."

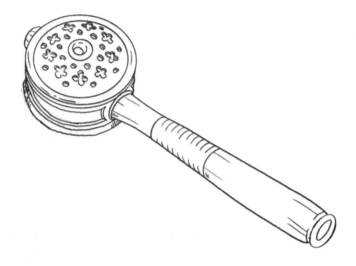

Benjamin had made the wooden rattle. He had hollowed out the wood and carved intricate designs on the surface. He had placed dried peas inside to produce a pleasant sound. Afterward, he secured the handle and presented the toy to the little princess.

* * *

The foal's four legs wobbled as he stood up. Ari and Gunther exchanged glances and patted each other on the back. But the little guy stepped backward and fell.

"Gunther, that makes six Edelross foals. We need another mare to continue to grow the bloodline."

"I agree but getting the mare here is the hard part."

"Let's talk to Johann about exchanging our original mare for a different one from King Stefan's stock of Edelrosses," Ari said.

Gunther cupped his chin with his hand. "What if a guard rode the mare to Herrgott and returned with the new one?"

"That could work," Ari replied.

A horse whinnied in the background, capturing Gunther's attention. "Are you ready to saddle break the oldest foal? She's the right age."

"Sure," Ari said with a cute grin. "My method or yours?"

"Your method," Gunther replied, "but we'll skip the first lesson." Ari frowned. "I don't want to be tied up in leather straps and listen to gibberish."

Ari gave him a puzzled look. Then he remembered Benjamin's and Klaus' first lesson on his farm. "Good idea." Ari replied with a wily grin. "You're a bright student. We'll begin with lesson two. By the way, do you have a girlfriend?"

"Girlfriend? What does that have to do with saddle breaking?"

"You'll see. Let's get started."

Johann came out to see his father, but what he saw made his eyes shine. "Are you two going to saddle break today?" he asked.

"Yes," replied Ari.

"Do you have a girlfriend, Gunther?" Johann asked.

"What's with the girlfriend?" Gunther asked again.

"You'll see," Johann replied, winking at his father. "By the way, the courier entourage is leaving for Herrgott in the morning. Is there anything you need before they start their journey?"

"Yes," Ari replied. He walked closer to Johann and shared

his thoughts of trading a mare.

"This is a wise thing to do," Johann agreed. "I'll share this with Albert. By the way, Anna was asking about her pawpaw this morning."

Ari smiled, but let it slip as he looked at the horse he was going to saddle break, the first Edelross born in Christana. "I can't help but wonder...will this horse miss her mother if we take her back to Herrgott? Will the mother miss her?" Ari muttered softly. "Lesson two is supposed to be fun. Time to focus on this beautiful young mare."

Ari entered the corral and ambled toward the mare. After the horse nodded, Ari turned his back and walked away. He approached the mare several times and turned his back intentionally ignoring her. Then the horse started to follow Ari when he walked away. Gunther rolled his eyes and gave Ari the thumbs up signal. "I get the girlfriend joke."

* * *

Melted wax puddled on the folded paper. King Albert lowered his seal in the sticky substance before it dried. He handed Stefan's letter to the courier and watched him place it in his pouch. Eight guards mounted up and started their journey south. One of them rode a mare.

* * *

"Petra, your letters are on their way," Ivar shared. "It could be two weeks or more before we hear a reply."

"Soon enough." Petra replied. "I should be finished with this blanket by then."

"It's beautiful. Let me guess. It's for Anna?"

"Well, I don't think it's for me," Ari said, entering the cooking room. "Hi, Ivar. Good to see you, Son." Ari paused as his eyes fixated on the embroidered outline on the blanket. "That looks familiar."

"I copied the design from your banner. I'm presenting the blanket to Anna on her baptismal day."

"Well done, Petra. This blanket will keep her safe and warm," Ari said.

* * *

The rushing water warned the guards that the converging river lay ahead. Rubbing his shoulder, the courier moaned as watched the water flow downstream. His hand subconsciously pulled the strap of the letter pouch over his head. Suddenly, a hawk swooped down with extended claws. Full of fright, the courier raised his arms to cover his face. The pouch fell from his lap and spilled open littering the ground with its contents.

Watching the hawk fly away, the captain of the guard yelled at the courier, "Hurry up."

The excited man gathered the letters and stuffed them back in the pouch, noting that the wax-sealed letter was among the group. In his haste, the courier had accidently missed one hidden letter behind a protruding rock. Back on his horse, the courier placed the strap over his shoulder and nodded.

The guards slammed their heals into the horses' flanks. Their mounts' eyes grew wild in pain and they protested with loud neighs. Dust flew in the air as the group galloped away. From out of the woods, a finely dressed man rode by where the courier had fallen. One of his guards accompanied him. Something white on the side of the path caught Falke's attention and had the guard pick it up.

With his hawk perched on his gloved hand, Falke read the letter and rolled his eyes. The everyday chores of a woman held no interest to him until he saw two words: blanket and minister. Falke read it again. *Could the blanket be for a baby? A baby related to a minister, who is the brother of Johann, the prince of Christana?*

"Hmm," Falke uttered as he refolded the letter. "I will have this letter delivered to the recipient, Angela."

Back in the castle, Falke called for his trusted scout. Lochen approached Falke with apprehension. He never knew what mood his master was going to be in, and he tried to make himself small and nonthreatening. "Lochen, I want you to dress in common clothing and deliver this letter to Angela. Ask around if you can't find the address."

"Yes, Falke," Lochen replied relieved that it was a simple task.

"I want you to stay in the city and observe any unusual activity near the palace. Have some men stay on the other side and watch the trail day and night. Have them report to me when the courier proceeds back north."

"Right away, Falke." Lochen took the letter and left.

"I've been a patient man, and I can wait a little longer. The reward is worth it," Falke muttered.

* * *

"Lord," King Stefan exclaimed looking upward and clutching his letter. "I want to see my great-granddaughter. I want to see my family."

"Sire," the Head Counselor said, overhearing his king, "this is a dangerous decision. Our kingdom is safer if you are here. You can't go near that hawk castle. If he sees you, he might–."

Stefan threw his hand up and cut him off. "I missed Tea's wedding; I'm not missing Anna's baptism. I want to hold my great-granddaughter. I'm tired of living in fear. In the Bible, Johann (John) stated in his letter to the early churches: *There is no fear in love. Perfect love drives out fear.* That is a promise! God loves His family, and I love mine. And I have decided to let God drive out my fear."

"If you go, we need an illusion that you're still in Herrgott," one counselor suggested.

"We could make a proclamation that you are gravely ill, Sire, and ask the citizens to pray for you. Everyone would understand why you would be kept out of the public eye," said anther counselor.

"Especially the owner of the castle. It's a believable ruse," said the Head Counselor. "But, to get you out of the palace, you'll have to change your appearance."

Cocking his head toward the Head Counselor, Stefan narrowed his eyes forcing his furrows to dig in deeper. "What do you suggest?"

"Shave your beard and wear a guard's uniform?" he replied in a nervous tone.

Stefan stroked his beard. "I'm going to miss it," he muttered.

* * *

Greta's eyes sparkled as she read the letter to Tobias. Their daughter's writing style made them feel they were right there with her. "Petra has talent for writing interesting sentences."

"Perhaps she could write stories for children," Tobias added.

"On one condition," Greta began. "We get a copy of the book."

Tobias roared with laughter. "I have two amazing women in my life."

* * *

Angela brushed the hair from her face with her free hand. Her fingers cramped from the weight of the water bucket that pulled on her other hand. She gave a soft sigh after she laid the bucket down on the floor. Rubbing her aching fingers, she glanced at the table and saw her name on a letter. Her eyes beamed as she read her message, especially the part about visiting Christana and meeting a minister. "I've never been out of Herrgott before. I hope I can go."

"Go talk to your Uncle Tobias," her father said. "He may be able to help."

Tobias listened to her request. "Let me talk to the guard in charge when I go to work tomorrow. Maybe, he will let you go with them."

Angela prayed for the rest of the day. When she got up in the morning, she prayed again. She must have worn God down, because the impossible happened. The head guard agreed to her request, but she had to wear a guard's uniform and cut part of her hair off to make it look more like a man's haircut.

"How short?" Angela asked. "Hair can grow back, but this opportunity may never happen again."

The day before departure, Angela entered the servants' entrance with her Uncle Tobias. Lochen noticed the young woman coming to work. At the end of the day, he saw Tobias leave but not her. *Maybe she's required to live at the palace*, he thought and dismissed the whole incident.

Early the next morning, the detachment guarding the courier mounted their horses. The captain of the Christanan guards eyed his charges, the mare, and "new replacement guards." Two of the original guards were from Herrgott, and they stayed at the palace. He took in a deep breath as he weighed the responsibility of this mission. After saying a silent prayer to God, he faced his group and gave the signal to proceed.

The river offered no harm, but the woods were dense. The guards scrutinized the trees and bushes looking for a possible ambush at any time, but they saw nothing unusual. Clear skies and pleasant temperatures accompanied them all the way to Christana.

The town square came into view causing the guards to sit taller in their saddles. After they entered the courtyard, the gates closed. Several sentries watched the group as they stood guard on the ramparts while their hands rested on sword hilts. Sensing no danger, they relaxed to give the illusion that all was well for the benefit of the townspeople.

As soon as the announcement was made about the arrival of the courier guards, Maria, Albert, Tea, and Johann hurried to the courtyard. When they heard they had two new guards in the group, Tea passed Anna to Johann and ran with her mother.

"Did he come?" Maria anxiously asked.

"I hope so," Tea responded.

Maria scanned the group. "Papa!" She ran to him. Tears ran down Stefan's face as he hugged his daughter.

Tea rushed to their side. "Pawpaw!" Her grandfather moved his arm and hugged both of them.

"Great-pawpaw," Johann said carrying Anna.

Stefan raised his arms and looked up to the sky and said, "Thank You, Lord. I praise You for this wonderful family reunion." Stefan cradled his great-granddaughter in his arms admiring her precious face. "Tea, she's beautiful."

After the royal family entered the palace, the captain of the guard took the other "new guard" to a room near the palace gate and handed her a bundle of clothes. After changing, Angela asked, "How can I find a man called Ivar? He's a minister."

The guard pointed toward the nearest building. "Probably in the church." The guard spoke both languages fluently.

"That will be easy to find," she replied. "Thank you for bringing me here. I'll be forever grateful."

"King Stefan is the one to thank. He's the one who gave the permission to bring you. When I presented your request, he immediately said yes. He said that he would like to have 'an angel' accompany the group. I may have mispronounced your name, Angela." Then, he winked at her.

Angela thanked the head guard once again. This time, he accepted her gratitude. *I need to find my cousin,* she thought. *The minister can help.*

As Angela was walking to the church, Ivar spotted her. "Petra, you cut your hair!" Angela remained quiet as she walked closer. Ivar's eyes bulged. "I'm so sorry! I thought you were someone else."

She smiled. "I'm Angela. Petra's my cousin."

"Angela? You came. I'm so glad to meet you." He studied

her. She sure did look like Petra, like a twin sister. He introduced himself and offered to take her to the other minister, because she kept asking for him.

Entering the church, Magnus saw the two. "Petra, you cut your hair!"

"Magnus, Petra did not cut her hair," Ivar corrected.

"Ivar," Magnus replied as he walked closer to his brother, "it's shorter."

Magnus stopped walking, his heart started pounding, and his face brightened. "Hello, I—I..." he stuttered.

"Angela, this is my brother, Magnus, the other minister. Magnus, this is Petra's cousin, the one with the pretty eyes."

"Please to meet you, Magnus," she replied in Christana's language.

"You know our language. Pleased to meet you, Angela."

"You must be tired from your journey," Ivar said.

"I'll take you to Petra," Magnus jumped in. "You can ride my horse. Ivar, I'm going to borrow your horse. Okay?" And the two of them walked out the door.

"Do I have a choice?" Ivar muttered, watching them go. "You have it bad, Magnus."

Riding past the barn, the house came into view. "Petra!" Angela yelled.

Petra dropped the bowl she was holding and ran to the yard. Angela dismounted and ran to meet her cousin. Magnus watched the cousins and noticed how similar they looked. *The one with the short hair is mine,* he thought. *I hope she'll be mine.*

After the two ladies hugged, they walked over to Magnus as he tethered the horses' reins. Petra put her arm in Magnus' arm. As he turned to look at her, Angela put her arm in Magnus' other arm. Both escorted him to the house. Ari watched the whole performance from the barn. "Hmm, thank you, Lord!" Ari reached for his locket and proclaimed, "Johanna, our family is growing. Another daughter."

Chapter 27

The Enemy Comes in Like a Flood

Sweat beaded on Lochen's forehead. Taking a deep breath, he entered the dimly lit chamber and reported to Falke. "Nothing? You found nothing unusual?" Falke stood up and kicked his chair. *Could I have been deceived?* he wondered. Narrowing his eyebrows, he glared at his scout and questioned him again.

Lochen shifted uneasily while unconsciously wringing his short stocky fingers. "Several days ago, there was a young woman who went to the servants' gate, but never left at the end of the day. I never saw her again."

"Maybe," Falke paused and pursed his lips in thought. Lochen recognized that look and remained quiet.

The letter on the path. It invited the owner of the letter to come for a visit. Could this be the servant girl going to the palace? Falke thought sporting a snide grin. *There's one way to find out.*

"Return to the home of Angela and ask for her. If she's not there, find out where she's staying. Say you have another letter for her. Take a horse this time. I want a quick reply."

"Yes, Sire." Lochen bowed his head and slowly backed away from his master grateful to have a chance to appease him.

* * *

Word reached Falke's ears that his scout had returned from Herrgott. Falke eyed the doorway waiting for the report. Lochen walked in holding up a fake letter. "Falke, her parents said that Angela would be gone for a month or more. She went to Christana."

Falke leaned back in his chair. An eerie glare washed over his eyes. The scouts he had set to watch the woods walked in and broke his concentration.

"What did you observe?" Falke asked.

"Just the same number of Christanan guards that came through the path as before," one of the guards said. "We stayed a little longer to see if a Herrgott group would follow."

"Was there anything unusual about the guards?" Falke asked.

"One of them looked rather old for being a guard. He was quiet."

"Where there any females with them?" Falke pressed on.

"Female guards? That's funny, Falke. Really funny," the Falke guard replied and laughed. "No female guards."

Falke dismissed them all except for Lochen. *Really funny,* Falke repeated the words in his head. *That's why I'm sitting in this regal chair and you're not.*

Falke turned his attention to Lochen. "Prepare yourself for another trip. Take the path that you have been using on this side of the river deep in the woods so the ferryman and Herrgott guards won't see you. Go to Christana and report back to me. Be careful; continue to be silent. Your knowledge of Christana's language is good, but your accent will betray you. I don't want any attention drawn to yourself."

Lochen nodded to Falke and left immediately for Christana. He scouted the town for several days and went back and reported to Falke. "The royal family is gathered together for the baby's baptism, Sire."

"Is King Stefan there, too?"

"Definitely," the scout confirmed. His black eyes glistened knowing Falke would be pleased with his report. "Once the entourage reached the palace in Christana, the word spread quickly. The school children saw a much older king in the courtyard. Several of them told their parents. I heard his name mentioned many times."

"Did anyone notice you?" Falke pressed on.

"I don't think so. I wore their traditional cloths, and no one paid any attention to me. Even if I wore different clothes, I don't think anyone would notice."

"Why do you think that?" Falke asked as he leaned toward his scout.

"There's much excitement in the town about the new baby."

A snide grin appeared on Falke's face. *This is the opportunity I have been waiting for,* he thought. "Is it a boy child or girl child?"

"A girl child, Princess Johanna."

"You have done well, Lochen. We must go and pay our respects, too. This child may be our sovereign someday. King Stefan is old and will need an heir to the Herrgott throne."

"Inform the men to make preparations for travel," Falke ordered. Paying his respects wasn't Falke's intent, but it seemed like a logical reason to tell the men why they'd go to Christana.

"Yes, Sire," Lochen said. Bowing his head, he indulged in the fact that he was Falke's most trusted confidant.

"This will be my finest hour," Falke boasted. "My years of planning are coming to an end. It's time to act."

Falke gathered his men together. "Gentlemen, there's a new royal born about three to five days walk from here. Many people are going to pay their respects. This royal is related to King Stefan. There's a rumor that some people want to hurt this family. We've been asked to supply protection. Let's go pay our respects and protect this family. We'll need to take our weapons with us. Take your swords, bows, and arrows."

The men lifted their voices, "God save our king." Falke turned his head and wrinkled his face into a tight smirk.

"Lochen, walk with me," Falke commanded. The two men returned to the empty throne room. Lochen's eyes widen as his master lowered his voice and revealed his true objective.

Stepping slightly back, Falke continued, "To accomplish

this move, we need to walk to Christana. It will take longer, but fewer horses make less noise. This group of ragtags will never see the truth. I'll tell them a credible lie when we get there."

"I've not forgotten your faithfulness, Lochen." Stepping closer, Falke whispered in his scout's ear. Then he stepped back to watch Lochen's face. The scout's beady eyes widen and his mouth drew into a tight smile. "Good, then we're agreed."

Falke had one more item to attend to, his hawk. He gently stroked his bird. "I can't leave you behind."

* * *

Ari's family brought the banner blanket to the palace. Anna cooed and held the blanket to her face and stared at the cross on it. Petra beamed. *She likes it. Anna likes my gift.*

Josef picked up the rattle that he and his father had made. Benjamin and Meta watched their son hold it close to Anna. The baby reached for it and grabbed it from his hand. Anna cooed every time she heard the rattling noise. Josef watched Anna in her baby cradle while the grownups talked.

"Meta, you've been a blessing. Thank you again for teaching the children. I hope you'll take my place again."

Anna continued to rattle her toy. Swinging her arm sideways, she hit the wooden edge of the cradle. Startled by the noise, she cried. Immediately, Tea bent over and picked up her baby. Anna still cried.

"Her rattle broke," Josef said looking at the scattered, dried peas.

Tea tried to pry the rattle from Anna's fingers, but she held it tightly. Meta offered her another toy. Anna spread her fingers out and reached for the other toy causing the broken rattle to fall into her mother's lap.

Josef frowned as his picked the peas out of the cradle. Visions of helping his father putting them in the rattle caused him to sniffle. *Maybe Papa can fix it.* Josef tucked the dried peas into his pocket.

Anna closed her eyes and fell asleep as Tea soothed her baby. "Good idea, Anna," Ari whispered. "Let's all go and get some rest. Tomorrow is Anna's special day, her baptism into the promises of the Lord."

Anna couldn't sleep that night. When Tea held her, she stopped crying. When Tea put her in the cradle, she cried. "Maybe she's uncomfortable," Tea said.

"Maybe she's spoiled," Johann added.

"Let's put another cloth in her cradle and see if that works." Anna continued to cry. Tea blew a puff of air trying to get a strand of hair out of her face. "Put another cloth down, Johann."

Anna still cried. Finally, after five cloths, Anna smiled and went to sleep. Tea and Johann quietly tiptoed to their bed. Anna slept all though the night for the first time.

* * *

Magnus and Ivar took turns reading from the Book of Services for the Baptism of Infants. King Stefan stood as the male witness and Meta stood as the female witness. Meta treasured the honor to be part of the royal family on this day of baptism.

Laying in Meta's arms, Anna never fussed or cried. *I'd give my life for her,* Meta thought as she held the little baby.

Ari's and Benjamin's family accompanied the royal family into the palace for the midday meal. Josef watched Anna wherever she went. By the time they walked to the palace, she had fallen asleep. "May I put Anna in her cradle?" Meta asked.

"Yes, please." Tea graciously accepted the offer. "I want to spend time with my grandfather."

"Can I go, too?" Josef asked.

Tea nodded. Josef quietly clapped his hands and smiled. *I get to be with Anna.*

As the family prepared to sit down, a commotion arose

outside. One of the guards came rushing in and announced, "Sire, we're under attack!"

"What do you mean?" King Albert asked sternly.

"Sire," the guard continued, "The horse gate was opened for only a moment and many men wearing hawks on their tunics came rushing in from the woods. Some on horses. Some on foot. The courtyard gates are still holding but not for long." Everyone's face turned pale.

"It's him," Maria said. "He's here!" The dreaded moment had arrived. "Papa!" Maria exclaimed, looking at her father.

"It's all right, Daughter," Stefan said calmly. "I'll go talk to him."

As Stefan finished talking, another guard came rushing in and said, "They're killing our guards."

Albert immediately addressed Johann, "I know this man. He's unstable. Has been for years. Your daughter's life could be in danger. Get her out of the palace."

Benjamin stood up. "Johann, they'll be looking for royals, not commoners. Meta and I could get Anna safely away from here."

"God be with you. Go!" Johann ordered.

Benjamin rushed down the hallway to find Meta. His heart raced with each step he took. Thoughts about what to do with his own child tormented his mind. At first, Meta balked at her husband's idea but reluctantly agreed. She reached down and cupped Josef's face in her hands. "Be brave, my son. Jesus is with you." Tenderly she kissed her son and let Benjamin take over.

Benjamin looked into his son's eyes as he got on his knees, "Josef, this is very important. I want you to quietly hide under the bed. I'm taking Mama to her sister. Can you be a big boy and do this for your papa?" The bewildered boy nodded. Benjamin hugged him. "Good, now hide. Remember, quietly."

Meta put on her old cloak. Covering up Anna with the blanket that Petra had made, she carefully placed the sleeping baby under the cloak. She held her midsection pretending she was with child.

Looking at the empty vestibule, Benjamin guided Meta through the door and hurried to the front gate just as the hawk guards broke down the horse gate. One of the intruders saw them leave and ran toward their direction. As soon as the couple entered the town square, Benjamin grabbed the first horse he saw and put his wife in the saddle. A hawk guard grabbed Benjamin from behind. "Ride!" Benjamin yelled.

Another guard on horseback chased her, but Lochen yelled, "We don't need her. Look at her clothes. She's a commoner. This one we'll take inside."

Benjamin twisted and pulled, but the guard held tight.

Several hawk guards rushed into the dining hall and ushered everyone outside to the horse pasture. The remaining hawk guards stood on the ramparts with Christana's guards kneeling in front of them. Falke placed his hands on his hips as he waited for his captives. He noticed Gunther and yelled at him, "Saddle up my horse, the white one."

Stefan approached the hawk man. Two hawk guards pointed their spears, but Falke raised his hand and shook his head. He sneered at Stefan with contempt and walked around the king, mocking him. "You don't look so powerful now. You thought you could get past me, old man? You've kept these horses from me all these years, but you would gladly give them to Albert anytime he wanted them. Do you think that castle was enough to placate me?" Falke exhaled loudly out of his flared nostrils in front of Stefan.

Falke walked over to Tea and studied her face. "Maria, I haven't seen you in years. Your daughter looks just the way you did the last time I saw you."

Next, he turned to Albert. "We used to be friends at one time, remember?" Albert held his tongue not wanting to further infuriate his adversary.

Falke found a new target. "Ari, father of Magnus, Ivar, and Johann. You must be very proud of your sons. The good Lord sacrificed His Son. Which son would you be willing to sacrifice?"

Turning to the other women, Falke continued his attacks. "Ah, Petra and Angela, you almost look like twins. Cousins, correct?" His eyes narrowed on Angela. "The female guard I presume?"

Falke strutted around pleased with the power he had over the group in front of him. "Bring the horse here," Falke ordered the caretaker. Gunther reluctantly guided the stallion to where Falke stood. "I knew I could get you to work for me one way or another. If you would have accepted my offer years ago, you wouldn't have that scar."

A hawk guard approached Falke. "We couldn't find the child."

Tea closed her eyes, gave a quiet sigh of relief, and said aloud, "Thank you, Lord."

That caught Falke's attention, he walked over to her, and yelled in her face, "Where is she?"

Johann struggled against the hands restraining him. He yelled, "She doesn't know, and neither do any of us."

At that moment, Lochen approached Falke and whispered in his ear. Falke gave a snide grin.

"I believe you," Falke calmly answered back. He turned to look at King Stefan. "See, old man. I *can* believe. What do you believe? Some invisible hand is going to come down out of the sky and save you? Now, that's funny." Falke paused with a deep breath contemplating his next move. "I will be the ruler of Herrgott, and I'll leave no stone unturned to prevent anything from getting in my way."

Falke mounted the white Edelross. After he fastened the leather glove on his right hand, he asked for his sword and clinched it in his left hand. Someone let the hawk go, and the bird landed on the gloved hand. The startled horse flinched and snorted, rolling his eyes at the dangerous bird next to his body.

Falke looked at Benjamin. "They don't know where the child is, but you do. " Falke faced Tea and edged his sword toward her body.

Stefan immediately charged forward with his hands up in the air. Recognizing the signal, the Edelross reared up on his hind legs.

Falke dropped his sword to free his hand. It hit the horse on the way down and cut his rear leg. The horse kicked his hind legs, trying to attack the object that had injured him. Falke lost his balance and fell out of the saddle releasing the bird as he hit the ground. The horse's front hoofs came down and trampled Falke in the chest as he lay helplessly on the ground.

The horse that the hawk man had coveted so much for all these years would be the instrument that took his life.

Gunther grabbed the reins and pulled the Edelross away. King Stefan ran to the hawk man and called him by his proper name, "Stefan, Stefan!" The elderly king knelt next to the injured man and held his hand.

"I'm scared. I'm losing control," the hawk man cried as he writhed in pain. "I'm going to die! I don't want to die!"

Ari and Johann gave each other a puzzled look. "Falke just threatened Tea. Why is he comforting this evil man?" Ari asked.

"Stefan, you're mortally wounded. You are going to die." King Stefan paused and took a deep breath. "There's still time. Give your life to Jesus."

"He wouldn't want me." The hawk man struggled to talk. His lung had been punctured by a broken rib.

"Stefan, you are my only son. I love you. You just talked about the Lord sacrificing His Son. He loves you, and His sacrifice is for you, too."

The hawk man looked up at Gunther and expressed his sorrow. "Gunther, I'm so sorry I hurt you."

"You're forgiven," Gunther replied. "I forgave you years ago. I'm at peace. Give your heart to Christ, Stefan. He's a good God."

"Maria, my baby sister, I'm so sorry. Please forgive me," her injured brother said with deep regret.

Choking back her emotions, Maria managed to nod at her brother but remained silent.

"Papa," the dying man said as he looked into King Stefan's eyes, "I'm ready." Magnus and Ivar stepped forward and led the dying man in the sinner's prayer, and the Lord immediately, with His sovereign Hand, set Stefan the Younger free and wrote his name in the Lamb's Book of Life.

"Papa, you're right," Stefan the Younger shared with a new Spirit in him. "It's wonderful. I see Him. I see Jesus. Everything is beautiful there." Slowly, Stefan the Younger turned his head toward Tea and Johann. "She's safe; Anna is safe. Do not worry." He looked lovingly at his father one more time, closed his eyes, and passed away.

King Stefan bent over and wept for his son. He wept for his life, he wept for the reunion with his son, and he wept for joy knowing his son was with the Lord.

When Falke died, the hawk guards threw their weapons down and put their hands over their heads except for Lochen.

Magnus and Ivar grabbed the man's arms and forced him to move.

The palace guards quickly stood up, recovered the discarded weapons, and escorted the intruders to the middle of the pasture. Albert ordered them to sit on the ground until he and Stefan could assess what to do with them. Fortunately, the first guard's report was incorrect. Only a few guards suffered wounds, but no one had lost their life except for Stefan the Younger.

Johann had not known the connection of the hawk man to Maria. Although Gunther knew, he had never told Ari. His loyalty to Maria and Albert prevented him from sharing that information.

Turning to her husband, Tea pleaded, "Johann, go and bring our daughter home."

"Where is she, Benjamin?" Ari quickly asked.

"Meta headed to her sister's village, Geir. She's riding a horse with Anna tucked inside the cloak she's wearing."

"That's a long way north from here," Ari said. "We should be able to catch up with her before she gets there."

"We'll need food and milk. Anna will be hungry soon," Johann added.

"I'm going," Benjamin said. "My wife is out there along with Anna. I'm going to get Josef. He's hiding under the bed. As soon as I talk to him, I'll be ready."

Ari, Magnus, and Ivar, all wanted to go with Johann and Benjamin. Ari and the twins had been through the northern region many times selling horses and knew the roads and villages.

Johann held Tea in his arms and assured her, "We'll find our daughter."

"Johann, my uncle said Anna was safe, but I have a terrible feeling about this." Tea choked back her tears. "I want to believe she's all right."

Johann gathered his beloved in his arms and comforted his wife. "Doubt can overshadow faith, Tea. I see her as being safe.

Feelings can waver and deceive us. I believe. Have faith with me."

"I will trust in the Lord," Tea said as best as a mother could who doesn't know where her baby is. She kissed her husband, reached for the locket that covered her heart, and placed her faith in God.

The journey to bring Meta and baby Anna back home began.

The Victory Belongs to God.

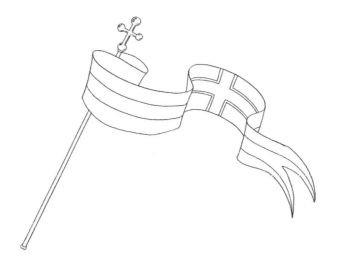

Exodus 17:15 – Jehovah Nissi, The Lord is my Banner.

The journey concludes with part three of the trilogy:

Journey in the Waiting

Chapters   *Discussion Starters*

1. What happened to Ari that helped him change his life?

2. Why didn't Ari's worst fear materialize?

3. What is the importance of Johann giving away his locket?

4. Why did Benjamin and Klaus want to go to Ari's farm?

5. How does Klaus demonstrate his ability to take care of the farm by himself?

6. In what ways do King Albert reach out and help Johann'?

7. How does Benjamin react to the unknown and Falke's behavior?

8. What misunderstanding did the innkeeper have with Benjamin's food order? Have you had someone to misunderstand you? How?

9. Why did Johann have to talk to the counselors'? Have you ever been put in a similar situation? What happened?

10. For what reason did Ari raise his hands?

11. Why did Ari admit that he was a bully? What benefit happened after his admission?

12. Compare letters written 400 years ago to letters written today. How are they different? How are they the same?

13. Why did Gunther have to forgive the man that hurt him?

14. How do you get respect from someone? How did Ari get Gunther's respect?

15. How did Tea get the students to participate?

16. Why did Ivar go to the King Stefan? Have you ever had a similar experience? Explain.

17. Describe Falke's character.

18. Why did Albert tell Ari about Falke? When have you sought help like Albert did?

19. What character traits did the counselors use for selecting new guards? Why are they important?

20. What is important for a good foundation in a home?

21. Why did Johann have to wear a disguise?

22. Why did Jesus have to die?

23. How would you describe Petra? What are her priorities?

24. What did Tea wear on her wedding day? Why?

25. Why did Tea choose the name Johanna for her daughter?

26. How do you drive out fear?

27. What is the sinner's prayer? Why was Falke's name included in the Lamb's Book of Life?

What will happen to Meta and Anna in the next book?

Acknowledgements

Journey to the Noble Horse, has been an honor to write. Sometimes, it felt like I was taking dictation rather than writing. The beginning was set by Book 1, *Journey to the Glass Hill,* but everything after that was unknown. I had no outline in mind. Without the Lord guiding me, there would be no story. Therefore, He gets the glory.

All three books in the Journey trilogy are written with the goal of offering wholesome and inspiring reading entertainment. Being a teacher, I incorporated scriptures, prayers, and faith as a learning tool for the reader. The questions at the end of the chapters are there to facilitate family discussions.

My Beta readers were indispensable. They gave their sound advice about the plot and characters as well as pointing out grammar and spelling errors. The ages ranged from 12 to 66 years. Natalia Billings, Miguel Billings, Lynette Nelson, Kathy Maske, LJane Mason and Denise Daniels.

A special thanks to Kathy Maske and Denise Daniels for reading Book 1, *Journey to the Glass Hill,* to their students (4th and 5th grades). During the middle of the book, COVID 19 of 2020 cancelled on campus school attendance. The rest of book was recorded and presented on LOOM for classroom instruction.

The illustrations in each of the chapters are the gifted handiwork of Rev. Brian King. He gives a visual representation of the characters and artifacts in the story. He also illustrated *Journey to the Glass Hill.* Deborah Jayarathne crafted the cover of the book displaying the running horse. She also designed the cover for *Journey to the Glass Hill.* I am forever grateful for their talents to get the images just right.

Gene Baker, my editor, is so gifted at finding the weak

areas, vague information, and missing details in my writing as well as all the grammatical and spelling errors. With his knowledge and careful eye, he makes the story better than I could hope for. He is not only a great editor, he is a great teacher.

In Chapter 13, the ABC's of Giving your life to Christ is by Fred Winters who was slain while teaching a sermon one Sunday in his church. At the end of each service, Fred always offered an Altar Call. He shed tears for those who walked up and shed tears for those who didn't. Fred was a mighty man of God. He used alliteration for his sermons outlining the main points. Fred's best alliteration is: Exalt the Savior, Equip the Saints, and Evangelize the Lost. It's inscribed on the back of his gravestone. You can find him on YouTube sharing the Good News about God.

About the Author

D Marie has taught school for over thirty years. She incorporated various educational methods to develop the joy of reading. D Marie designed this inspirational book as a learning tool to nurture Christian character and living. Her first published book, *Journey to the Glass Hill,* is the beginning of the trilogy. The conclusion of the Journey trilogy is *Journey in the Waiting.* D Marie lives in the Midwest with her husband and family.

www.DMarieBooks.com

Artists

Illustrations: Brian King is the Pastor of Family Ministry at the Lutheran Church of Webster Gardens in St. Louis, Missouri. Reverend King also drew the illustrations for *Journey to the Glass Hill.*

Cover Design: Deborah Jayarathne. She also designed the cover for *Journey to the Glass Hill.*

When there seems to be no way, what do you do? *Journey to the Noble Horse* is an inspirational story of two families whose lives intertwined four-hundred years ago in a heartfelt journey of faith, family, and forgiveness. Ari came from a modest family of commoners, but King Albert's family ruled Christana. The Lord's plan brought them together just in time to weather a coming storm that would threaten to turn their lives upside down. A mysterious man, known only as Falke, had plans of his own concerning Ari and King Albert. As Falke's growing power began to unfurl, emanating from his ominous castle on the Herrgott River, he began to intrude more and more into the life of each member of the families, flaunting his resentment, anger, and revenge. Only by leaning on the Word of God and prayer will each family member grow enough in their faith to overcome the challenges that await them.

Journey to the Noble Horse begins where *Journey to the Glass Hill* ended. Johann, Magnus, and Ivar had all left home on the same day. King Albert welcomed Johann into his palace while Magnus and Ivar headed south to Herrgott. Ari, their father, sat alone in his home grappling with his personal behavior and the knowledge that he had driven his sons away. He had always been in control, now he controlled no one. For the first time in his darkest hour, he turned to prayer. Could the Lord provide for him?

These hope-filled novels are designed to be learning tools to uplift the reader in their Christian walk.

Made in the USA
Coppell, TX
14 February 2023

12796655R00132